White Flight

A Novel

Peter O'Keefe

UNCOMFORTABLY DARK HORROR

Book Cover Design and wrap by Don Noble of Rooster Republic. House image used with permission of the artist, Sally Young

Cover Image © Sally Young, *House Painting Number 3*, acrylic and mixed media on board, 2022.

First edition 2025

Original content editing by Gabino Iglesias

Final editing & formatting by 360 Editing, a division of Uncomfortably Dark Horror.

Editors: Candace Nola & Mort Stone

Published by Uncomfortably Dark Horror, owned and operated by Candace Nola. Pittsburgh, PA

Follow us on all social media, our Patreon, or on our website to stay up to date on new releases, appearances, and more!

Committed to *"bringing you the best in horror, one uncomfortably dark page at a time."*

Patreon

Website

ter in a tragic accident. A display of love so well-meaning that it becomes caustic, and even with the best of intentions, every decision they make leads to something more horrific than they could ever imagine. Peter O'Keefe's book will wreck your soul, and you will stand up and applaud him fiercely for doing so!" — Jill Girardi, Author and Owner of Kandisha Press

"A brutal look at the tensions of American racism, O'Keefe's White Flight is a lightning-paced haunted house tale that asks hard questions. The novella holds up a mirror to white America. Those brave enough to look are in for a hell of a ride." —Elizabeth Broadbent, author of BLOOD CYPRESS

To Lesley, who is always there for me.

To my brothers Michael O'Keefe and Dennis O'Keefe, who will always live in my heart. And because it makes me happy to see their names in print.

Special thanks to Gabino Iglesias for his editorial insight and support at a time when I really needed it.

White Flight

Willow opens her eyes with a start. The dream was so vivid, so real, she has to lie still for a moment to convince herself she is actually awake. Unfolding herself from a tight fetal position and sitting up, she realizes she's fallen asleep in D's bed again. And, as usual, she has no memory of coming into the room.

It was one of those dream cosmologies where the landscape of the waking world was detailed with absolute convincing clarity. Everything looked right. Everything was in its proper place. But it was all somehow wrong. She was standing just inside the front door. On a suffocatingly dark night. There was no one on the street, no lights in nearby homes. The world was emptied out of everyone but her.

And there was a T-Rex on the porch. A black T-Rex. *And yes, she thinks, D went through her dinosaur stage, so I know what a T-Rex looks like. Well, almost; it was small enough to be standing on my front porch, right? It was maybe somewhere between the size of a raptor and a T-Rex, actually. A compact car version of a T-Rex? Perhaps a young T-Rex? And why was it black? Didn't D paint her little plastic T-Rex black when she was small?*

The creature was standing at the bottom of the porch steps, but it was so massive it had to duck in order to poke its flaring nostrils against the screen door, like a cartoon cat sniffing outside a mouse hole. She was afraid it would eat her, so she took a step back. That's when she saw the man in a hoodie standing on the lawn next to the porch. He was freakishly tall, thin, pale, dressed in black. He was in charge of the T-Rex.

"You need to let him in," he said, smiling. His air of cloying reassurance reminded her of the obsequious director at the funeral home.

She was amused by his request. "You mean I need to invite it in? Like a vampire?"

The beast remained calm, its broad snout pressing up against the door like the prow of a ship. She marveled at the jagged rows of crocodilian teeth. She didn't know T-Rexes had crocodilian teeth.

The tall man spoke again. "Let him in. He will find your daughter. He will find D."

Willow immediately opened the door and stepped to the side. The beast lowered its head and squeezed through the doorway, moving past her without a sidelong glance. The man on the lawn looked at her with concern. "I think you better come outside."

She went out onto the porch and watched as the creature moved off into the house, dumpster snout pressed to the ground like a bloodhound. She turned to her bleak companion. Somehow, instinctively, she knew he was the devil. But she didn't care. His beast was going to find her daughter. He was going to find D.

But then, it all went to pieces.

Willow sits rigid on the side of the bed. She grips a fistful of hair in each hand and pulls on it until it hurts. Then, she keeps pulling. D is not missing. D is dead.

———

The gritty neighborhood of tree-lined streets is one random island in the vast archipelago of urban enclaves scattered across this rust-belt city. The staggered rows of century-old homes have long served as one of the city's bulwarks against the ravages of time. But now—hammered by relentless waves of tumult and decline—the ranks of red brick structures have been decimated by shotgun patterns of vacant lots marking the sites of demolished homes.

The gaps between the houses are somewhat softened by community gardens and vibrant murals. Among those still standing, recently renovated homes with late-model SUVs in front stand shoulder to shoulder with ramshackle wrecks with bedsheets for curtains. On the nearby avenue, a food co-op and a hipster coffee house have planted their flags amidst the payday loan shops and the storefront churches. The liquor store is boarded up, and there is a "For Rent" sign in the dusty front window of BBQ Brothers Righteous Ribs. This is a neighborhood in transition.

A burly two-story brick home commands one street corner like an ivy-encrusted blockhouse. Like every other house still standing in this neighborhood, it is a seasoned survivor—pitted, scarred, and possibly maimed—in its own particular way. One of the oldest homes in this part of the city, the once proud structure has, over time, been divided into flats, abandoned, burned, boarded-up, squatted in, wrapped in crime tape, and, eventually, reclaimed as a single-family home.

The six-foot wood privacy fence encircling the yard like a stockade is of recent vintage. The freshly tiled roof feels like a temporary patch, capable of being sloughed off by this glowering monolith with one angry shrug. The manicured lawn in front of the house further differentiates it from some of its more downscale neighbors. Planted dead center in that tidy green plot is a "For Sale" sign. An "Under Contract" placard hangs beneath it.

The structure itself, suffused in the dark weight of its history, has calcified somehow. The individual pieces of wood, brick, plaster, cement, copper pipe, tarpaper, and glass—assembled by long-dead craftsmen into something in the shape of a house—have been forged by time and tragedy into one solid, hulking object with the density of a tombstone.

A freight train is moving along the railroad tracks that bisect the neighborhood like a zippered scar and pass directly behind the corner house. Inside the house, Joel Ward gazes out over his farmhouse sink as the setting sun is reduced to rapid staccato flares between boxcars. Every object in the kitchen vibrates as several hundred tons of steel and freight rumble across the raised earthen berm less than a hundred steps from where he stands. Eventually, the clatter of stacked plates and windowpanes is reduced to mere tremors before dissipating completely as the train snakes away to the south.

Joel turns away from the window to lean back against the quartz countertop. He is a man in need of a good night's sleep. The shirt and trousers look to have been reclaimed from the laundry hamper, and his once neatly trimmed beard is an untended shrub. The iridescent-blue

Warby Parker eyeglass frames only manage to accentuate his pasty complexion.

The eyes behind those glasses stand in sharp contrast to the rumpled exterior. Exhaustion has fractured his usual aura of control, providing a rare glimpse at the barely contained ferocity within. There is a grim history of brokenness here. A brokenness that, like the house, has only been roughly mended.

Momentarily calmed by the slushy wump-wump of the Bosch dishwasher, he inventories the kitchen. The espresso machine is a solitary, gleaming gargoyle on the once cluttered countertop. The colorful Le Creuset cookware is packed securely into cardboard boxes, and the refrigerator has been stripped of its magnets and photos. The floating shelves above the stainless-steel appliances are empty. Only the most frequently used pots and utensils continue to dangle from the hanging racks over the custom-built center island.

Feeling wistful, Joel rubs the sole of his shoe across the polished maple floor they'd refinished after excavating it from beneath a dozen sedimentary layers of linoleum.

If only...

Then, he realizes that a covered pot on the stovetop continues to rattle long after the train's departure. This is nothing new. They've awakened in the middle of the night to the sharp clanging of radiators, in a house where they were stripped out by scavengers years before. Doors don't stay shut. The floor behind you creaks beneath the weight of trailing footsteps in an otherwise empty room. Objects dropped on the floor routinely defy the laws of physics. Padlocks open by themselves.

Recalling these incidents, Joel is more pensive than afraid. The strange phenomena seemed harmless, almost comical, when D was alive. She'd laugh at them for being so skittish, secure in some intuitive understanding of the occurrences that filled her parents with such dread. Her fearlessness, her giggling dismissal of these manifestations, reassured them—made living in this oppressive pile bearable, fun even.

That child. That remarkable child. Our child. But now she's gone.

His musings are cut short when he looks at the stove to see water spitting through the gap between the pot's lid and the rim. He realizes the pot is merely boiling over and turns off the burner.

Joel leaves the kitchen. He strides through a canyon of moving boxes in the dining room and into the adjoining living room before stopping. He stands there and listens. There it is: that muffled, vaguely organic, impossible to source sound. In the beginning, it was a tinny rasp, so faint as to be almost indecipherable, like the buzzing of a wasp trapped between the panes of glass in a distant window.

They spent weeks trying to track it down. It was so indistinct yet so all-encompassing they were convinced it must be something behind the walls. They brought in pest control. They ripped out plaster walls and wood lathe, pulled up carpet, and knocked holes in the ceilings. In the end, baffled, they'd given up. They came to accept it as some innate property embroidered in the very fabric of the house—the default background texture to the home's intermittent eruptions of ghoulish instrumentation. They decided to live with it. They didn't really have a choice.

Just like that damn room upstairs.

The neat stack of photo albums on the coffee table suddenly collapses into a disordered mound. One of the albums slides off the edge of the table and flops open on the floor, exposing a sheet of faded black and white photos with scalloped edges. The images capture a Black family from an earlier era celebrating a holiday meal in the adjoining dining room. Joel kneels by the table and closes the album, revealing vintage beadwork on the cover spelling out the words "The LeFlore Family." He reorders the clunky tomes into several smaller stacks less likely to fall prey to the home's peculiar properties. Finished, he moves into the front entrance hallway, plants himself at the base of the stairs, and calls up to the landing. "Pot's boiling over."

There's no answer from Willow, so Joel trudges up the stairs to the second floor. He strides down a long narrow hallway, closed doors to either side, footsteps echoing off the refinished oak floorboards. Barak Obama's screen-printed visage proclaims "Yes We Can" as he passes, while colorful Juneteenth, Kwanzaa, and Italy travel posters compete for attention.

The door to the rear corner bedroom is ajar. There is an open padlock hanging from the hasp bolted to the doorframe and Joel briefly examines it before going inside.

Willow is perched on the edge of the bed, her slight form barely creasing the taut, Black Girl Magic duvet cover. She has the dazed look of someone just awakened from a deep slumber. Her shoulder-length hair, limp and rapidly advancing from blonde to white, is in sharp contrast to the exuberant halo of curls framing the smiling face of the Black girl on the duvet. Willow's pale skin is nearly translucent, revealing a thin latticework of delicate blue veins. She looks as if, seen in the right light, she'd be transparent.

The curtains on the windows have been taken down but the shades are drawn. The room itself resembles a museum dedicated to the memory of one particular child. That child—adopted, Black, female—peers out at them from a succession of photos: from squirming toddler to boisterous, radiant young girl, to sullen teen.

One framed photo captures much younger versions of Joel and Willow at the adoption ceremony. The two very new, very white parents are flanked by a grinning judge and a somber social worker. Willow is gripping the bawling Black infant as if she were a newly recovered meteorite that has not yet cooled to the touch. Joel looks stupid happy.

Joel eyes his wife with concern. "You okay?"

"Please stop asking me that."

"Okay...Alright..."

There is a moment of strained silence.

"I just...I thought you didn't like being in here on your own."

"Don't."

He's perplexed. "Don't what?"

She's glaring at him now. "Just. Don't." She turns away, muttering under her breath. "I'm not doing this anymore. I'm just not doing this."

He takes a ring of identical keys out of his pocket and tests one of them in the padlock. It works.

She avoids looking at him when she speaks. "It wasn't me this time. It must have already been unlocked."

He removes the key from the lock. "I know." He jangles the keys before pocketing them again. "I keep them with me all the time. It's just..." He sighs, defeated. "It's just this damn house, I guess."

Willow, her attention focused on the contents of the room, is no longer listening. "I'll never understand why she insisted on having this room. After everything...The things they say happened here." There's something approaching awe in her voice. "I mean, from the first time she set foot in here. She just couldn't. Not. Have. This. Room."

Joel flips absently through the framed posters stacked against a wall—Megan Thee Stallion, Beyoncé, Nicki Minaj—taken down to make room for the photo array. "New drywall. New flooring." He shrugs. "Next to the bathroom." A weak smile. "Furthest from our room. She was a teenager after all."

She turns to him in astonishment. "My God, Joel...We found syringes under the carpet. And that...that vile, horrible graffiti."

"It wasn't graffiti. It was..." He stops himself, realizing that the alternative is even worse. "Whatever."

"Blood."

"We don't know that."

"It was blood. A lot of blood."

He's determined not to go there. "Who the hell knows? The whole house was a smoking wreck. Remember when we landscaped the yard? Could have sold the shell casings by the pound."

She flinches when he releases the stacked posters to clatter back against the wall.

"Sorry."

He moves to the dresser to examine a cardboard box crammed with objects retrieved from a sidewalk shrine. There are stuffed animals, slumped candles, photos, fliers, and rain-spotted sympathy cards. The entire boxed bundle has been encased in a clear plastic trash bag.

A photo enlargement pressed up against the plastic depicts their daughter shortly before her death. She is light-skinned, with the barest hint of freckles. Brown, almond-shaped eyes hint at some Native American ancestry. Although her hair has been shaped into an afro that accentuates her height, her shy, almost childish smile makes her look even younger than sixteen. The photo is covered with scrawled hearts and messages from well-wishers.

Joel grips the sides of the dresser and stares unhappily at the collection of artifacts. Willow seems to read his mind. "It was a nice gesture. They meant well."

"We didn't even know most of those people. It's just...morbid."

Willow is already disengaging, her voice dreamy. "And all that food. I don't think I can even look at another sweet potato pie if I live to be..." Her voice trails off.

"What a waste. Who could eat at a time—?"

"I told you we should have donated it."

He turns on her accusingly. "Did you have the energy for that? Did you?"

She looks away.

"Didn't get out of the damn bed for a month." His manner softens, and it looks as if he is going to reach out to her, to comfort her. Instead, he turns back to the dresser. "Not that I blame you. It's just, they never reached out to us before. Before..." He grows silent, unable to bring himself to put the horrifying reality of their loss into words.

After a moment, he regains his voice. "And the way everyone acted. So Goddamned entitled. Like she belonged to them. Not to us. Her parents. Her goddamned parents. They didn't even know D." More softly. "Not really. Not like we did."

They are quiet for a long time. She's smoothing the already perfectly flat duvet, picking off even the tiniest hints of pilled fabric with her fingers. He's toying with a small assemblage of basketball and soccer trophies arranged on a shelf.

When he finally turns to look at his wife, the bravado is gone. "How did we...When did we lose her?"

Her voice is kind now. "She just needed time to figure things out. That's all she wanted." She struggles to produce a tiny smile. "Just time."

The words come out much louder than he intended. Almost a shout. "Figure what out? Goddammit! What? What was there to figure out? That she couldn't come to us? That she couldn't..." The words being formed in his mouth disintegrate into nothing more than a long, wet sigh.

She doesn't have an answer for him. He grips a soccer trophy as if he's going to throw it, then carefully returns it to the shelf. "Sorry."

She's annoyed. "Stop saying that. Stop apologizing all the time."

He nods and fusses with the trophies. "Gonna have to start packing all this up pretty soon."

"I know. Just let me have a little more time to..."

He turns and grabs the memorial box from the dresser.

"What are you doing?"

He puts the box under his arm and opens the closet door. "I don't know why you have to take this out and torture yourself."

She looks to Joel, startled by his assertion. "Joel...I..."

He stops. "What?"

She looks away, her voice barely a whisper. "I thought you..."

"What?"

"Nothing. Never mind."

"Oh." He carefully sets the box back in the closet and closes the door. Then he remembers his purpose for being there. "Pot was boiling over."

"Did you turn it down?"

"I turned it off. I thought..."

"Never mind. It's fine." She rises wearily from the bed. "I need to go make dinner." She pauses in the doorway to press her fingers against the hand-painted sign tacked to her daughter's door, directly above the Black Lives Matter bumper sticker: "Black Queen."

After she leaves, Joel moves around the room examining random photos. Most capture D at various stages of childhood in their former suburban neighborhood: youth sporting events where she is the rare person of color; holidays, surrounded by Joel and Willow's white extended families; in a backyard bouncy castle with a platoon of white cousins.

One photo memorializes D as one of four grinning Girl Scouts seated at a table outside a grocery store hawking Girl Scout cookies. Joel never noticed the body language apparent in the image before this: the three white scouts sit shoulder to shoulder on the right of the frame, leaving a slight but visible gap between themselves and D, already conspicuous due to her height and dark complexion.

The next photo on the wall captures twelve-year-old D posing sheepishly, hands clasped in front of her, beside the array of poster boards displaying her science fair project. The project her mother insisted she pursue, over the objections of both D and her teacher. D's brief was to map out the entire triangular slave trade route between three continents. She—or more precisely, her mom—calculated the distances, the prevailing currents, the average speed of the sailing vessels, the estimated weight of their human cargo, and the average time it would take to cross the Atlantic. D didn't earn any ribbons.

The outside world bursts through the window in the form of a passing freight train, releasing Joel from the room's spell. He goes into the hallway and shuts the door behind him. He secures the door with the padlock and moves to the hallway window just outside the bedroom to watch the train pass.

There is no train. The railway berm is empty. Joel looks around in confusion as the shaking briefly intensifies before slowly resolving. He takes another puzzled look out the window and heads for the stairs. Inside the room, after his footsteps have moved off down the hallway, D's adoption photo slips from the wall and crashes to the floor.

Joel has just started down the stairs when there is a knock on the front door. He hurries down the steps, eager to atone for his paralysis with the boiling pot.

"I got it."

He grabs the reproduction vintage brass doorknob and opens the door. There's no one there. Joel unlatches the screen and peers out. There's no one on the sidewalk. He steps out onto the porch and looks both ways down the block. The street is deserted. He turns and goes back inside the house.

Willow is chopping green onions on the kitchen counter when he enters. "Who was it?"

He shrugs. "Nobody there."

"That's odd."

"Probably those kids again."

"You shouldn't be so rude to them."

"C'mon, who goes door-to-door selling candy with nothing but a pocket full of loose, dog-eared candy bars? How can that possibly be legit?"

"You exaggerate. Besides, it's not easy for these kids. Especially the boys. With even the well-meaning white folks giving them the fisheye."

"What's that supposed to mean?"

Willow ignores him. She goes to the stove, takes the lid off, and stirs the pot with a wooden spoon.

He's not ready to let it go. "I raised a Black child. Remember?"

She stops mid-stir. Rigid. "We. We raised..." She pauses for emphasis. "A child."

He flaps his open hand at her, in what could be interpreted as a conciliatory gesture. "We never had D knocking on people's doors hustling candy bars. That's all I'm saying."

She gives him a sharp look. "No. Kids at the Triumph Academy Charter School don't go door-to-door selling candy bars for their sports teams. They go on fully chaperoned environmental field trips to Costa Rica." She replaces the lid harder than necessary.

"And they go to college. Good colleges."

"What does that matter now? What does any of that...?" Growing distraught, she abandons that line of thought and busies herself at the sink. "Maybe she'd have been better off knocking on doors. None of the other kids in this neighborhood attend the charter, and they seem to do just fine. She never had any friends here."

"She had friends. Lots of them. At school. A solid, hard-working, academic peer group. Like we talked about."

She turns to face him, her back to the sink. "Why did we even move here? Wasn't that part of the plan? Giving D the opportunity to live in a Black neighborhood? In a Black city?"

"We did everything we could to—"

She rolls right over him. "Even after we moved here...summers were soccer camp. And science camp. And band camp. And the whatchamacallit...Coding camp. And then the charter downtown..."

"The integrated charter downtown. That you helped choose. Remember?"

"Mostly white and Asian."

"Thirty-two percent Black and Hispanic."

"In an eighty-five percent Black city. She didn't know anybody here in the neighborhood. She didn't get a whole lot of..." She does air quotes. "Black culture."

He holds out his hands in a conciliatory gesture. "We were just trying to give her every opportunity. Every advantage. All the things she never would have had if she'd—"

"If she'd what?"

"Don't you go there. Don't you even dare go there."

She can't meet his gaze. She turns off the stove and pours the potatoes into a strainer in the sink. She stands there, hands gripping the porcelain lip. He goes to join her by the sink. She gives no indication that she even knows he's there.

They stand side by side in silence, staring blankly out the kitchen window. There is a narrow alley between the rear fence line of the yard and the rail embankment. To the right is the house next door. To the left, a quiet side street emerges from beneath the rail overpass. Something has caught Willow's attention, and Joel follows her gaze. There is a reddish glow brightening the sky above the rail embankment.

"Looks like a fire on the west side. A big one."

Joel grabs utensils from a drawer. "What else is new?"

Willow's cell vibrates on the counter next to her. She checks the display while drying her hands.

Joel is setting the table for dinner. "We're just getting ready to eat."

She puts the phone to her ear and moves past him into the dining room. "Hi, Jacob."

He calls after her. "You could at least put it on speaker so I can be a part of this conversation."

She ignores him and walks through to the living room. He stands in the kitchen doorway and watches as she takes a seat on the couch.

"Oh, of course. Thank you. I appreciate your saying that." She reaches out with her free hand to grab one of the old photo albums stacked neatly on the coffee table. "Yes, I've got them right here. Oh, that's okay. I can find some boxes to put them in." She smiles, being silly.

"We are practically boxed in by boxes of boxes here these days."

Joel has taken a seat at the table by the time she returns to the kitchen.

"He'll be here in another hour or so."

"Did you tell him this is not a particularly good time? Considering..."

She goes to the counter and begins to plate their dinner. "When is it ever going to be a good time?"

"You could have shipped them. That's all I'm saying."

She brings two plates to the table and sets one in front of him.

"It's already dark. Why can't he come some other time? For Christ's sake, the closing is next week."

She settles into the seat opposite him. "He works. This is the only time."

He picks up his fork. He attempts to make it sound like a joke. "You really are becoming a couple of besties, you two."

"He seems like a nice man. I'm happy to do it." She gazes wistfully in the direction of the living room. "A lot of those pictures were taken in this house. It looked so different in those days. So full of life. He must have so many stories." She turns to look at the sink on the back wall. "I always knew the kitchen must have been added on to at some point."

"What does he really want?"

"I've already told you. He grew up in this house. He wants to see it again. And he wants those family albums. I mean, who wouldn't? They're an incredible—"

"After all this time?" Pausing with a forkful of food in the air, he nods his head in the direction of the living room. "If those were so goddamned precious why'd the family leave them to rot in the basement?"

"Nobody knew."

"Nobody cared."

"His grandmother was in a nursing home when she passed." She gives him a pointed look. "When we bought this house."

"We didn't know that. It was a tax sale." He pokes at the food on his plate. "How were we supposed to know that? And where was the rest of her family? Where the hell was Jacob?"

"I don't know. Let's just not talk about it anymore, okay?"

"Did he not know what was going on? Or maybe...maybe he just wasn't in any position to do anything about it."

Willow responds heatedly. "Sure, he's Black. He must have been incarcerated. Right?"

"I'm not saying it's fair—"

"Not in the military. Not hitchhiking across Europe. Not just a typical—if he was white—irresponsible young guy too busy having a life. Or, maybe, just one of a million other things we just don't know about."

"I'm not saying it's because he's...It's just, growing up in a neighborhood like this...Like it used to be, I mean. In poverty, so to speak. It makes a big difference. That's all I'm saying."

"From what I understand, this used to be a pretty nice neighborhood, which happened to be Black, historic even."

"He's not coming all this way for a bunch of old photographs. He wants to guilt us into selling him the house. Not that I blame him, the way property values around here—"

"Would that be so bad?"

"We have a buyer. Cash offer. As opposed to his FHA loan. With contingencies. That we've already rejected."

"It's so depressing—they'll probably just tear it down—combine it with the lot next door and knock it all down. Build more condos like they're doing all over around the university now."

"Why should we care? We'll be gone."

"I don't know." She sets her fork down with a sigh and gazes out the back window. "In spite of everything, this house has such good bones, such potential. And I'm not just talking about financially."

"We talked about this. We're going to move on with our lives."

"There's so much history here. Sometimes, I feel as if we've only scratched the surface..."

"Fairy tales. That stuff about the Underground Railroad, the Orphanage...Never happened. You know that."

She turns wistful. "I was talking to the mailman...The neighbors, they still call this the LeFlore house."

"Yeah. And at one point they called it the flophouse. And then they probably called it the drug house. And then it was that old burned-out house on the corner. And the murder house. The death house..."

"Stop."

He leans across the table, determined to make his point. "You know, I have roots in this city, too. My grandparents lived not ten blocks from here."

"That was a long time—"

"Raised a family. Lived and died here. I belong. We belong."

"Then why are we leaving?"

There is a loud knock at the front door. Willow starts to get up. "Might help if you fixed the doorbell."

Joel pushes his chair away from the table. "Sit down. I'll get it."

J oel hurries through the house to the front door and opens it, ready for a confrontation. The porch is empty. Joel clambers down the front steps and crosses the lawn. When he gets to the corner, he does a 360 on the sidewalk. Nothing. No one.

"Son of a bitch!"

He hurries back across the lawn and peers into the gap where the driveway separates their house from the one next door. The narrow space between the two homes is dimly illuminated by light leaking through the kitchen curtains. The neighboring home is dark behind drawn window shades. The far end of the driveway is blocked off by the wooden gate leading to Joel and Willow's yard.

Joel checks to make sure that the side door to their house is locked. Then, he walks up the driveway and reaches over the top of the privacy fence to confirm that the gate is latched on the inside. He strolls back out to the front lawn and takes a moment to study his surroundings. The rest of the block, a hodgepodge of brick homes and the occasional vacant lot, is mostly dark.

He crosses the lawn to check their car parked in front of the house—replacing the garage was going to be the next thing on his to-do list—but the Subaru appears to be undisturbed, the security light blinking serenely on the dash. It seems strange not to see Willow's Toyota parked directly behind it, but she does nothing but Uber now. Ever since that night. Ever since D...

He looks toward the avenue a few blocks distant and remembers being excited when they first moved in to see a green roof on one of the storefronts. Things really are looking up in this part of town. Closer inspection revealed it was an abandoned structure with weeds and junk trees sprouting from the roof gutters. He shakes his head at the memory. Talk about naïve.

He turns to go inside but stops for a moment to study the white flag announcing their unconditional surrender: the "For Sale" sign. He sets the "Under Contract" placard to wobbling with a gentle tap and mounts the steps to the house.

Willow is clearing the table when he returns to the kitchen. "What did they want?"

"Nobody there."

"Seriously?"

He shrugs and moves to the sink. "I'll do the dishes."

"Why would someone do that?"

"Guess I should have bought those candy bars."

"Do you think somebody's harassing us? Could it be because of D?"

"That's done. Over with. The circus has already moved on to the next town."

"Maybe it's got something to do with what's going on over on the west side right now? You know there was that other one...a young man."

"It's kids. Don't worry about it. What I can't figure out is how they're getting away so fast. Where the hell are they hiding?" He sees her take a concerned look out the window. "It's probably just the kids next door messing around."

"There are no kids next door. That was the previous tenant. It's an older couple, for a while now."

"Oh, right, now I remember. Hard to keep track, living next door to a rental. Aren't they moving out already?"

"Yeah, little by little it looks like. So now we'll get to live next door to a vacant house again."

"Not for long."

"I still don't get it. Why are they evicting them just so they can have one more vacant house on the block?"

"They're not getting evicted. They can't afford the rent anymore."

"Now, no one will be paying rent there. How does that make any sense?"

"It's an investment property. Once the neighborhood picks up a little more, they'll flip it, or knock it down, or whatever. Whoever owns it—the university, some investor—they'll get their money back. With room to spare, I would guess."

Willow picks up a dishtowel and starts to dry. She smiles as she recalls a more pleasant memory. "Remember when D found that waffle iron stuck way back in the cupboard? Had to be fifty years old if it was a day."

Joel nods happily at the memory. "Keep meaning to get that rewired. Bet it still makes a damn good waffle."

"And all those patent medicine bottles holding up the shelves in the basement? Remember? What did we ever...?"

"Still think we should have uncorked one of those puppies."

She responds with shock. "The main ingredient on the label was chlorophyll!"

He's grinning, enjoying himself. "I tell ya, somebody was feeling no pai—"

There is a knock on the front door.

"For the love of..." Joel snatches a towel to dry his hands and sprints through the house to the front door.

———

J oel flings the door open and rushes out onto the porch. There is no one there. He leaps off the porch and charges diagonally across the lawn to the corner sidewalk. He does a quick 360 and scans all four intersecting streets. There is no one in sight.

Joel jogs back across the lawn toward the driveway and the gap between the two homes. He barrels around the corner of the house and stops. The house next door is dark with the shades drawn. He goes to check the side door to their own home. It's locked. Through a gap in the curtains, he can see Willow finishing up in the kitchen. He checks the gate to the yard. It's latched from the inside.

Joel walks back to the porch. He's completely at a loss; it just doesn't seem possible that someone could have knocked on their front door and disappeared so quickly. He cuts diagonally across the front lawn to the corner sidewalk again and looks around. There's no one on the street. There are no cars. Only the occasional backlit curtained window indicates any sign of life in nearby homes. The city feels abandoned. It's as if some secret distress call has been broadcast to everyone but them.

Then, Joel hears the distinctive whooshing rumble of a mechanized street sweeper. He turns to see the boxy silhouette of the machine as it emerges from beneath the viaduct. The sweeper moves along the side of the house, rotating wire brushes scouring the curb as it goes. He tries to get a look at the driver, but the headlights, mounted high on the grille, are blinding, and he's forced to raise his arm to shield his eyes.

He attempts to peer through the side window as it passes, but the cockpit is dark and he can see nothing inside—the machine could just as easily be driving itself. The motorized pillbox turns left at the corner and crosses in front of the house. Joel watches as the mechanical beast moves placidly down the street and disappears around the next corner.

W illow has settled onto the living room couch with one of the LeFlore photo albums nestled on her lap. Pressing her palms against the pebbled cover, she remembers her lingering fear that the infant D's birth mother would show up one day and take the child away. Still later, she suffered pangs of guilt when she found herself secretly hoping that someone would come and claim this bawling, colicky, stubborn child.

But she got through it. She taught herself—through trial-and-error, through guesswork, through research—how to manage her daughter's tough, unruly hair; about flat-irons, hair products, and shower caps. And, in the end, she reassures herself, *I...Well, we, raised a beautiful, loving, caring child.*

To be honest, it was more her fear of failure—the humiliation of having to admit she could not properly care for this child—that drove her in the beginning. Joel, aside from being a cheerleader, was basically useless until D was old enough to appreciate his dad jokes. And her family...*Well, she thinks, they did eventually come around, didn't they? Mom was a trooper. And Dad...tried, didn't he?*

Willow's hands slowly curl into fists. *Why do I have to give them credit for making the effort to tolerate, eventually accept, and maybe, possibly, grow to love their own grandchild?*

She makes a conscious effort to unclench her fists, takes a series of deep breaths, and spends a few moments centering herself. Relaxed now, she opens the album with the care of an archivist examining a rare manuscript. She'd ignored Jacob's initial efforts to reach out because she had hoped to keep the photo albums for herself. The books were her personal portal into a happier dimension, a secret place where she could retreat to create an alternative history for her daughter. A world where D unambiguously and unapologetically belonged.

She turns the pages to admire Black families posing in their church finery in front of this very house. There are photos capturing gaggles of LeFlores gathered in the dining room for holiday meals. Others depict generations of LeFlore women, in previous incarnations of the kitchen, going about the hard work of feeding their families while chuckling at long forgotten jokes. They crowd around wide-eyed newborns in the living room and enjoy backyard barbeques where Willow once grew tomatoes and herbs in her raised planters.

There are school photos, church choirs, sporting events, Halloween costumes, and wedding receptions. There are presents piled beneath Christmas trees groaning under the weight of tinsel and ornaments. There is life. There is energy. There is love. In this house, in this bleak, soulless pile of brick, plasterboard, and impeccably refinished floors.

That was the life Willow wanted for D when they moved to the city. As a child in the suburbs, she wasn't just a Black child in a white world; she had the added misfortune of being big for her age and towering over her classmates. At three, other parents at the playground thought she was five. At six, they thought she must be at least nine or ten. By the time she turned ten, she was often mistaken for a teenager. A Black teenager.

That's when Willow finally warmed to Joel's plan to move back into the city where he was raised. She'd been skeptical of her husband's desire to buy and renovate a house in one of the city's up-and-coming neighborhoods but decided it was the right thing to do for D's sake. And it was actually closer to their jobs; hers at the university, and his downtown.

What wasn't clear to her was why Joel wanted to make the move. She sensed it was about something much deeper than fixing up some old, tumbledown house closer to his office. It was something he couldn't articulate even if he wanted to, and he grew defensive when she brought up anything beyond the practical aspects of the move. For Joel, the return to the city of his youth—much like his adoption of a Black child—seemed intended to make some sort of a point, to prove something to himself that even he only vaguely understood.

It would have been fine if they had chosen one of the more affluent, integrated neighborhoods where both they and D would have fit in. But Joel had caught the bug. *Goddamn HGTV,* she thinks. *Those damn shows have done more damage to this nation's psyche than Fox News! He was determined to renovate a house for us, to make it our own.* She snorts out loud at the memory.

"Our forever home." *Hah!* And those houses, at least the ones they could afford to buy and fix up, tended to be in the not-yet-gentrified neighborhoods in the city. Black neighborhoods.

The house he chose, this house, turned into a money pit. The basement was under water after the first rain, and they ended up replacing much of the foundation as well as the roof. The entire structure had to be re-plumbed, re-wired, and treated for lead paint and asbestos. The pipe connecting the house to the main water line in the street had to be dug up and replaced. They purchased paint, plasterboard, and drywall mud by the truckload.

But the floors, once sanded, were impeccable. And the house itself was starting to shape up into something really special. Something they could be proud of. It may even turn out to have been a good financial investment. Shortly after they closed, the neighborhood was "discovered" and—God, she always hated that word—gentrifiers began buying and renovating the dilapidated but basically solid 19th and early 20th century housing stock in this part of the city.

It was almost two years before they were able to move in, and D had already finished junior high in the suburbs. After checking out the local public high school, they ended up enrolling her in the Triumph Academy, a charter school that had just opened with great fanfare downtown. Joel dropped her off on his way to work every morning.

The Triumph Academy made all the upheaval worthwhile. Willow was thrilled by everything she saw at the charter. At the open house—unlike D's suburban junior high—there was a great deal of diversity. There were Asian students, Black students, white students, and Muslim students. There were Hispanic kids and East Indians.

The faculty and staff were equally diverse. And the parents she met were laser-focused on supporting the school's educational mission. Willow was positively over the moon for her daughter. D was going to blossom in this diverse, enriched educational environment.

Once school started, she couldn't wait to debrief D every night after dinner. Was she getting to know other Black kids? Who was in her class? Who did she talk to? Who was she becoming friends with?

D's reaction confused her. She deflected and parried her mom's questions until, finally; she ran out of patience. "Mom, I can't be your bridge anymore. I can't be anybody's bridge right now."

Willow stared at her daughter in bewilderment. "Bridge? What on earth are you talking about?"

Her daughter rolled her eyes, sighed deeply, and then spoke to her mother as if she were a child. "What I mean is, I can't be your racial tour guide all the time. That's not my job."

"D! That's a terrible thing to—"

Her daughter was adamant. "I'm not a bridge between the races, that's all I'm saying." She attempted to soften the blow with a sheepish smile. "Seems I need one myself half the time."

Willow flashed her best mom smile. She reached out to take her daughter's hand. "That's why this is going to be so good for you. You just need to give it a chance."

D pulled her hand away. "Just, please, let it go. Okay?"

"Sweetie, what's wrong? We thought you'd be so much happier with the charter, with all the diversity, being around other kids who look like you."

D stared at her mom as if she were speaking a different language. "Don't you understand? I'm still trying to figure out who I am. How I fit in. I don't even know how to walk into a room full of Black people. I can walk into a room full of white people. No problem. But now...It's like, I don't even know how to be Black. There's all these different kinds of Black people. So many different ways to be Black. I just can't..."

She tried to take her daughter's hand again but she pulled it away. Willow kept smiling anyway. "Just give it time, sweetie. You're going to be so good at this. You're going to make us so proud."

D's confusion turned to anger. "This is not about you. Or dad. Or whatever it is you guys think needs to happen. You need to see me. I'm not your pet, or your project, or your protégé. I'm Black. That's not ever going to change." She was glaring at her mom as she framed her own face with her hands. "This. Is. Who. I. Am."

Willow could no longer hide the hurt in her voice. "We know that. We've always known that, sweetie. That's the whole reason—"

"I'm Black and you're not. You have to understand that. No amount of your love or good intentions or wishful thinking or assimilating me to whiteness..." She grimaced. "Or dad's old white guy, up from the bootstraps, tough love lectures—"

"D! That's a terrible thing to say about—"

"—is going to protect me."

"Protect you? Protect you from what, sweetheart?"

D stood up so abruptly she tipped the chair over. She picked the chair up and leaned on the back, facing her mother.

"D, sweetheart..." The look of fury contorting her daughter's face abruptly stifled her.

"It just is what it is, Mom. Deal with it. Just...deal with it."

D threw the chair back down on the floor. She stomped up the stairs to her room and slammed the door shut behind her. She'd never done that before.

The next morning, Willow watched from the living room window as Joel pulled away from the curb on his way to drop D off at school. She was in the passenger seat, staring blankly out the window like a hostage.

W illow sets the photo album down on the table when Joel comes back inside. He closes and locks the door behind him. He stands there, grimly silent.

"Nobody there?"

He goes to look out the window. "No. Nobody."

She's skeptical. "You didn't see anyone?"

"What'd I just say?" He gestures angrily. "There's nobody fucking out there."

She goes to a different window and looks out. Her tone is conciliatory. "Probably just some kids playing games."

He's peering through the glass into the darkness. "Dangerous fucking game. Could get themselves shot."

She turns from the window, startled by his vehemence. "You would never do anything like that. Shoot someone."

He nods in the general direction of the street. "They don't know that." He joins her at the window and looks out. "We could be those people. Those people with the guns. Ready to shoot someone."

Willow looks at him as if he's suddenly become a stranger. "We've talked about this. There are no guns in this house. There will never be a gun in this house. Or any other house."

Joel moves to another window to look out. Willow watches him with concern. "Breathe. Do your breathing exercises."

He looks at her, annoyed, but says nothing. He tilts his head toward the ceiling and takes a series of deep breaths before responding. "Sorry, I'm a little on edge. This is just so..." He exhales deeply and moves to a side window with a view on the adjacent house. "Maybe you're right. Probably just kids."

Willow returns to the couch and sits down. She picks up one of the photo albums and presses it to her chest like a protective talisman.

He turns away from the window. "I'm going to get the flashlight."

"What for?"

He's already heading toward the basement door. "When they come back, I'm going to find out where they're hiding."

"And then what?" She rises from the couch. "It's upstairs. I'll get it."

He's peering out yet another window. "Why in God's name do you have it up there?"

Willow doesn't answer. She's already moving up the stairs, gripping the railing as if steadying herself aboard a ship on the high seas. At the top of the stairs, she pauses outside the door to the master bedroom. Before going inside, she looks to make sure that D's bedroom door at the other end of the hallway is still safely padlocked.

Willow closes the night table drawer after grabbing the flashlight. *This damn house,* she thinks to herself as she grips the textured plastic handle. *You've got to be careful to never drop anything anywhere. The pen, or the cap to the lotion bottle, or the can of pinto beans, or whatever the heck it is you drop, will invariably take a physically impossible bounce, roll in a complete arc around the room, only to drop onto the staircase where, instead of stopping on the top step, it will wobble like a possessed slinky down each and every step to the bottom landing, where it will, invariably, make its way underneath the couch, the stove, the water heater, or into some other nearly impossible to reach crevice.*

She grips the back of the chair at her dressing table until her knuckles are white. *This damn house.*

It was in the early days of her estrangement from D. In a rush to get ready for work, she'd grabbed a jacket draped over a chair. The hem of the garment somehow snagged the eyeglasses on her dresser, flinging them across the room and shattering the expensive prescription lenses against the wall.

D, passing the open bedroom door on the way to her own room, stopped when she saw her mother on her knees examining the bent frames to see if they were salvageable. It was the culmination of nearly a year of escalating household mishaps that had finally exhausted Willow's patience, and she turned to her daughter in tearful frustration. "It's this damn house!"

D eyed her with cool detachment. Her tone of voice was completely matter of fact. "House just doesn't like white people." She shrugged and continued on to her room, leaving her mother speechless.

Willow desperately wanted it to be a joke—that would have been so like D—but the chill in her daughter's eyes was unmistakable. She dropped the eyeglass frames into the wastebasket and finished getting dressed for work. Before leaving, she went and tapped lightly on D's door. She was met with silence. It would not be the last time.

In the final weeks of her life, D shut her mother out completely. Up to that point, Willow had felt a tinge of guilty pride that her relationship with D remained relatively close, even after their teenage daughter had mostly stopped speaking to her father. So, it came as a shock when D began to treat her with sullen disdain as well. How she had longed for one of those fleeting moments when teenage D allowed herself to engage in the sort of goofy amiability they'd shared when she was a child. But it was not to be.

Willow steps back into the hallway and is immediately immersed in the racket from an unseen train trundling by on the berm behind the house. She shuts the bedroom door and stands there for a moment to take it all in. The clamor builds in intensity until the windows are rattling and the floorboards are vibrating beneath her feet.

Willow can't help but smile, flashing back to a moment right after they had moved in when another passing train shook the house. D, already a teenager, had turned to her mother—eyes wide in mock horror—and shouted that they were under attack by a stampeding herd of dinosaurs. "Hadrosaurs probably!"

That little interaction had reminded Willow of the look of wonder on her daughter's face the first time they watched one of the Jurassic Park movies on video. Willow had chosen The Lost World because it was the one where Jeff Goldblum had the Black daughter. She thought D would like that, perhaps even identify with the Kelly character. Not that Joel is ever going to be mistaken for Jeff Goldblum.

All D cared about were the dinosaurs. And that was okay, actually. Willow was impressed by the little girl's ability to memorize not just the names—Velociraptor, Compsognathus, Gallimimus, Parasaurolophus—but also the most obscure factoids about dinosaurs and the distant eras when they walked the earth. And, in a sign of things to come, the child was outraged by the injustices inflicted on these majestic creatures by the movie's fictional baddies.

Willow realizes that the house is still shaking. *My God, this is a long train,* she thinks. The windowpanes are vibrating so fiercely she's concerned they're going to break. She's convinced there must be two fully loaded trains crossing paths directly behind the house on the dual tracks. But this level of turbulence usually only occurs in the winter when the ground is frozen.

Willow walks to the window at the end of the hallway just outside D's room. She grips the sill to steady herself against the rhythmic rocking and peers through the glass. The railway berm is silhouetted against the glow from the fires to the west. There are no passing trains. The berm is empty.

The tremors finally began to subside but the door to D's room continues to shake violently. The padlock rattles fitfully in its metal hasp before falling open. The door itself is bowing outward, as if struggling to contain an expanding mass from inside the room. The door frame is beginning to peel away from the wall, and the hinge pins are slowly bending in their brackets. Then, with one final convulsive lurch, the door is suddenly sucked back into place—as if by some powerful force from inside the room—and goes still.

Willow waits until the surrounding hubbub has dissolved into complete silence before approaching the door. She grips the handle and braces herself to open it. She switches

on the flashlight, and, for one glorious, effervescent moment, she is a warrior, arming herself with a light saber...No,
*dammit! I'm Ripley! With an assault rifle! Or driving that
futuristic forklift thingy. Ready to confront...confront what?*

She hears a metallic thud inside the room as one of the
framed photos crashes to the floor. Then, one by one, the
other pictures slam to the floor in a steady drumbeat of
tinny thumps and shattering glass. It's as if some spectral
figure is walking the perimeter of the room and knocking
each framed photo from the wall in turn. Willow's courage
evaporates. She releases her grip on the doorknob and
takes a fearful step back.

Joel calls from downstairs. "What are you doing up there?
Did you find it?"

Willow closes the padlock and gives it a tug to ensure it's
locked. She turns off the flashlight and moves to the stairs.
"Got it!"

W illow has nearly reached the bottom of the stairs
when there is a knock on the front door. Hard this
time. And then another. And another. These are solid, angry
blows, each more violent than the last. She stops so abruptly she slips backward into an awkward, half-seated slouch
on the steps.

Joel nearly crashes into the door in his haste to confront
the intruder. He turns to glare at her. "Why didn't you...?"
He mounts the first step and reaches out to snatch the
flashlight from her hand. He turns back to the door and
throws it open.

She calls after him as he bursts outside. "Be careful!"

Joel charges out the door, but there's no one there. He leaps off the porch and stumbles to his knees, the heels of his palms plowing the soft turf. He scrambles to his feet and sprints across the lawn to the corner sidewalk. He quickly scans his surroundings, but there's no one in sight. Joel hurries back across the lawn and into the void between the two houses. He targets the gate and then the side door with the beam from the flashlight.

Nothing. He turns and trots back across the lawn to the corner sidewalk. There's still no sign of any activity, so he walks along the street side, all the way back to the alley and the railway berm behind the house.

Joel paints the alley and the side of the rail embankment with the flashlight beam but finds nothing out of the ordinary. He grips the top of the privacy fence and pulls himself up far enough to shine the flashlight into the yard. He guides the circle of light across the grass, over the planters and patio furniture on the deck, and back again. The flickering cone of light reveals nothing but a handful of thin trees that would be incapable of concealing a fat squirrel.

Joel retraces his steps to the front of the house. After a moment's hesitation, he strides purposefully over to the neighboring house and knocks on the front door. There's no answer. He tries to look through the window, but the shades are down and the house beyond is dark. He tries the door. It's locked.

Willow is standing on the porch when he returns. "What were you doing over there?"

"I just wanted to know if they saw anything."

"I think they do shift work." She opens the door and moves aside for him to enter. "Come back inside."

He remains on the porch, smacking the flashlight into the palm of his open hand. "I'm going to find the son of a bitch if it's the goddamned last thing I do."

"Whoever it is, they're gone now."

Joel turns on the flashlight and checks his surroundings one last time. Then he follows Willow inside and locks the door behind them.

Willow hesitates, glancing nervously up the staircase to the second floor. "Did you hear a train go by? A few minutes ago?"

He's already hurrying over to one of the windows at the front of the house. "What train?"

Willow joins him as he peers through the curtain. "Just before someone knocked on the door, there was a train. Really loud. I mean, really loud!"

He's only half listening to her, still focused on the street outside. "I don't know. Maybe. There's always trains..." He suddenly backs away from the window, angry. "There's nobody out there! What in God's name is going on?"

"Maybe we should call someone."

"No. No police."

"I was thinking about one of the neighbors."

He's relieved. "Sure. Why not the Cavanaugh's?" He quickly backtracks. "No, never mind, they bailed. Got broken into again. Sold the house, 'As Is'. Don't think they even came close to getting their money back." He peers out the window. "I told them they should've gotten a dog."

Willow, arms crossed, hands gripping her shoulders, leans forward in an attempt to see what he's looking at. Joel turns to her. "We should get a dog."

She backs off, surprised. "You know D's allergic."

They both go quiet. Willow finally breaks the awkward silence. "I'm sorry, I forget. Sometimes it's almost like...never mind."

Joel can't meet her gaze—he doesn't want to go down that path. "There must be someone else. What about that nice lady down the street? The one you chat with on your walks? Used to work up at the rib place?"

"Bettina? I don't have a number. I don't even know her last name." She moves back to the couch and sits down. Her voice is plaintive. "We should have reached out more. It just always seemed there was so much going on. So many things we needed to do."

"We're not the damn welcome wagon. Besides, we go to all the potlucks. All that sort of thing."

"For the food co-op. No one around here shops there. It's for people like us. For other—"

"We're not gentrifiers. Alright?"

She nods, chastened.

"None of that was happening when we bought in the neighborhood. There was nothing trendy about buying here. The bank thought we were nuts. Remember?"

He gestures out the front window. "We invited people over for things. Nobody ever came." He sees her starting to respond and beats her to it. "Hardly anybody." His tone turns bitter. "Not till D...Not until after what they did to D. Even then..."

He shakes his head and moves to another window. "We tried to make a difference. We bought this house. Neighborhood fucking eyesore. Vacant for years. We put our savings, our sweat equity, into this damn place. Down to the studs. We shop local..." He throws up his hands in exasperation. "When we can." He gives her a pointed look. "I grew up here. And I..." He corrects himself.

"We. We were raising a Black child here." Thinking about D makes him angry again. "What about her? Did D not belong here? Tell me that."

Willow's voice is very small now. "Of course she did. I'm not saying that."

He moves away from the window. "Maybe it was a mistake, moving here. Buying this house. Things were just fine the way they were."

"No. No, they were not."

"What's that supposed to mean?"

"I never really appreciated how hard it must have been for her before. Before the move." She smiles; it's a good memory. "At first, she was so relaxed here. She wasn't always the one Black person in the room anymore. She could just disappear. Be average. Be normal. She didn't have to be special. She didn't always have to explain herself. But then, I don't know, something happened..."

"We let her move into that damn room. That's what happen—"

"She realized she didn't want to disappear."

"No, she wanted us to disappear."

"That's not true, Joel. That's not true at all. She was going through a rough time, working through some things. She didn't want to disappear. And she didn't want us to disappear. She wanted to be special. She wanted to make a difference. She was just beginning to figure things out. To accept, to understand how we fit in to all this..."

"We were her goddamned parents. That's how we fit in."

She ignores his interruption. "Trying to figure out how she fit in. Where she belonged."

"She belonged here. With us. In this house. Our house."

She rises from the couch and moves around the room, examining her surroundings, as if seeing it all for the first time. "It's just...I don't think it's our house anymore. Maybe it never was."

He'd be angry if he weren't so confused by what she's saying. "What the hell is that supposed to mean? I mean, sure...Once we close. But until then..."

She picks up one of the photo albums and studies it. She sounds wistful. "Seems like everyone on the block knew the LeFlore's. For most people around here, this still is the LeFlore house."

He turns on her in a rage. "Did anyone help out when the squatters came? The drug dealers? Did they come over with the gumbo and the guacamole and the sweet potato pie when there was a dead body rotting away in that room upstairs?" He stifles a sob, surprised by his own emotional reaction.

"In D's room?" He stares up at the ceiling in anguish, in the direction of the corner bedroom. "How did we ever even let her have that room? Knowing what we knew?"

She moves close and reaches out tentatively to him. When he doesn't pull away, she grips his arm in both her hands. "This house was abandoned for years. All those terrible things happened a long, long time ago. Any ghos—" She tries to make light of it.

"Any bedbugs, any bad mojo, any...whatever disappeared a long time ago. We completely renovated it. Like you said: down to the studs. Otherwise, we would never have let D move into that room. And remember, she decided. She wanted that room. She loved that room. It's almost as if she—"

She is interrupted by a loud knock. On the back door.

Joel yanks his arm from her grasp. "What the hell?"

J oel charges through the house to the back door. He flings the door open and runs out onto the deck. Seeing no one in the yard, he hustles over to check the front gate leading to the driveway and then the back gate. They are both latched from the inside. Joel opens the back gate and sweeps the flashlight beam up and down the alley.

Nothing! He walks the alley to the side street, skipping the beam of light along the steep slope of the rail embankment as he goes. Once he reaches the side street where it goes beneath the rail overpass, he can see that the fires lighting up the western horizon have spread. He turns away from them and walks slowly along the sidewalk toward the front of the house.

Willow stands by the couch and looks out the window as the beam from Joel's flashlight skitters across the tree lawn on the side of the house. Her phone vibrates on the coffee table. She looks at the screen and then picks up the phone. "Jacob? Where are you?"

Jacob LeFlore is parked on the side of the road. He has a door knocker goatee and close-cropped hair going grey at the temples. His lean, angular form commands the front seat of the Prius like a Muppet in a toy car. "Streets are all closed on the west side. Some sort of police action."

"Maybe you shouldn't—"

"I'm gonna try to work my way around. Just wanted to let you know I'm running late."

"There's really no need to come all this way. I can ship the albums."

"Can't do that." His voice is a smile. "Already promised my auntie I'd take her out for breakfast tomorrow."

"Alright but be careful."

"Shouldn't be a big deal. I still know my way around this town pretty good." He clears his throat. "Besides..." He lapses into silence.

"Yes?"

"I got something I need to tell you. Both of you. It's about the house."

"I don't understand. You haven't lived here in years." She puts her hand over the phone as Joel enters.

He looks at her in concern. "You're not calling the police?"

"It's Jacob."

He seems relieved. "Oh. Good. That's good."

"Jacob, I have to go. You be safe and we'll see you soon."

Willow ends the call and looks through the dining room toward the kitchen just as a clenched fist raps on the kitchen window closest to the side door. She cries out in terror. "Joel! Someone's there!"

Joel rushes to the side door. He struggles angrily with the chain lock before he is able to release it. Joel steps out into the gap between the houses. There's no one there. He steps out into the driveway and screams.

"Come out, you goddamn coward! What the fuck do you want? What do you fucking want from us?"

He checks the gate to the yard and finds it still latched on the inside. He turns and runs down the driveway and across the front lawn, swiveling the flashlight from side to side as he makes his way to the other side of the house.

Joel is winded by the time he reaches the alley. He can hear sirens in the distance as he stands with his hands on his knees to catch his breath. Looking through the railway overpass, he can see that the glow in the west has greatly intensified. This is clearly a major conflagration.

Willow is standing in the living room looking out a side window and watching the light saber of Joel's flashlight beam dance along the side of the rail embankment. She's trembling, trying to make sense of all this madness.

Why is this happening to us? Haven't we endured enough? With the loss of our sweet baby? The strain on our marriage? Walking away from all of the time and effort and money invested in this stupid house? Aren't we good people?

She laughs mirthlessly, reminded of something D once said to her. "AD" that is. The "After" D. As opposed to "BD," the "Before" D. AD was the "enhanced" version of D that was introduced into the world after she moved into that room upstairs. When she changed from a sweet, happy child into...into what?

Willow tried to be supportive, to be patient. She tried to encourage her daughter, to reassure her that whatever it was she was going through, it would all work out somehow. That she was a good person. D had looked at her mother with pity in her eyes. When she spoke, there was no anger in her voice, none of the snark Willow had come to dread over the previous weeks.

"Mom, the world does not give a shit if you're a good person or not."

Willow was too flabbergasted to even admonish her daughter for her language. She was inexplicably hopeful. Maybe the worst was over? Maybe she and her headstrong daughter were finally ready to emerge from this deep, dark pit? D, for the first time in what seemed ages, had actually called her mom.

Joel charges in through the front entrance and pounds the butt of the flashlight into the door after he slams it shut. Willow eyes him with concern. "You frighten me when you get like this."

He turns to face her, startled. "You know I would never hurt you. Either of y—" He catches himself before completing the thought. He comes into the living room and sets the flashlight carefully on the table. "Did you see the guy?"

"Just a hand banging on the window."

"White or Black?"

"What?"

"The hand. Was it white or Black?"

"I don't know; it was too fast; it was just knuckles." She's exasperated. "What difference does it make?" She picks up her phone. "This is getting ridiculous. I'm calling the police."

"And tell them what? Somebody's knocking on our door?"

"All the doors. And the windows now. Something's going on, Joel. Something is happening." Her voice is rising. "What are they going to do next?"

"Have you looked out the back? The whole west side is burning. The police are not going to have time for this petty crap."

"Look, I know you don't want to deal with the police. After everything...after D." She has to pause a moment to collect herself. "But there are times when we have no other choice." She tries to make light of it. "Besides, isn't it about time we used that white privilege D was always going on about?"

His voice is barely audible. "Fat lot of good it did her."

Willow's tone sharpens. "It's either that or leave and get a hotel room."

"No one's going to drive me out of my own goddamned house."

She stares at him, unsympathetic. "Weren't you the one wanted to move?"

"That's not fair—"

"Because of everything. Because—"

"Do you really want to stay? In this house, I mean? Not just tonight; permanently? After everything that's happened?" He gestures in the general direction of the street outside. "And now this?"

She stares blankly at the phone in her hand. She seems uncertain. "I...I don't know. I thought we were doing the right thing by moving, but now...I just don't know anymore."

He can't hide his astonishment. "What? What do you mean you don't know? You want to sell it to Jacob now?"

"No. Not Jacob. I'm just not sure we should sell it at all."

He stares at her in wide-eyed astonishment. "Why? What's changed?"

"It's just...everything's moving so fast. We've just been through—are still going through—a horrific, life-altering event. So maybe this isn't the time to make a major decision like selling the house we've invested so much time and money into. I just want to make sure we're doing the right thing."

He looks at her as if she's lost her mind. Then, he turns and walks into the kitchen. "I'm going to check the yard."

"Fine. I'm calling the police." She eyes Joel's departing figure warily as she dials.

———

J oel and Willow stand at the window and watch as two police cruisers arrive from different directions to park in front of the house. Joel is surprised by the response. "What the hell did you tell them?"

One cop gets out of each car. Both are white. Both are strapping men whose muscled bulk is barely contained by their uniforms and bulletproof vests. They have a brief, animated discussion before starting up the walk to the house. Willow eyes them skeptically before going to join her husband at the door.

"Why do cops these days always look like goddamned weightlifters?"

"Will..."

"What? They all look like they're on steroids or something. Why is that? It wasn't always this way."

"Maybe not where you grew up." He gives her a cautionary look before opening the door.

They both step out onto the porch to greet the two police officers. One cop, his shaved head reflecting the glare from the porchlight, can't seem to stand still. He moves onto the lawn and paces the perimeter of the flowerbed, shining his flashlight along the exterior of the house. The other cop, a stocky redhead, has the wispy beginnings of a beard that gives him the appearance of an apprentice Viking. Both cops seem surprised to find a middle-aged white couple standing on the porch.

Viking Cop stands with one foot resting on the bottom step. His manner is polite. "You the folks called this in?"

Joel, with a wary eye on Willow, takes the lead. "Wasn't sure we'd get someone out here this fast. With everything going on."

Bald Cop glances in the direction of the conflagration on the west side. "Burn the whole damn city down if you let 'em."

Viking Cop scans the surrounding houses before turning his attention to the couple on the porch. "This your place of residence?"

Joel's voice takes on an edge. "Do we need to show you I.D.?"

"Oh no, you're good. It's just, when we saw the address..."

Willow is immediately suspicious. "What about the address?"

Viking Cop clears his throat. "There was some concern this might be another one of those demonstrations. Civil disturbance maybe. Something along those lines."

"Why would anyone be protesting here?"

Willow realizes what he's referring to. "You mean the vigils?"

Viking Cop looks to his colleague for support but quickly realizes it's all on him. "The concern was...due to the incident with the young woman who used to reside at this address. The one who—"

"That 'young woman' was our daughter. She was sixteen."

Bald Cop whistles and rejoins his colleague. They look like two soldiers who just realized the path they're on is mined and they'll have to walk backward in their own footsteps if they want to get out alive.

Viking Cop is the first to find his voice. "Diamond Ward was your daughter?"

"Adopted." Joel starts to say something more, but the angry look from Willow stifles him.

Bald Cop is eying them with unabashed fascination. "That's right: they said the parents were white. Or mixed race. Or something."

"Maybe we should hand this off to a supervisor. Just to make sure..."

"We're good." The tilt of Bald Cop's head indicates the two people on the porch. "They took a settlement from the city."

"The city was supposed to keep that confidential. But the police union..." Joel clams up, realizing this might not be the most sympathetic audience for his complaint.

Willow grabs his arm. "Let's just forget it. Seeing the police cars will frighten off whoever's doing this. Sorry to have wasted your time, gentlemen. We'll be fine."

Joel is not having it. "We're still residents. And taxpayers." Willow grips his arm tighter, but he shakes her off. "I'm not apologizing to anyone. We dropped the wrongful death suit. We didn't want to profit off our daughter's death. We just wanted to get on with our lives."

"We need time for ourselves. We need time to grieve. We need time to heal."

"We're setting up a scholarship."

"Lawyers get it all anyway, right? That shyster of yours..." Bald Cop practically spits out the words: "Derek 'No Good Shoot Goes Unpunished' Porter. Wouldn't cross the street to piss on that son of a bitch if he was on fire."

"He's not our lawyer anymore."

"He didn't support our decision."

"No shit. Probably over on the west side right now signing up a new client."

"Joel, let's just go inside. We'll be fine."

Bald Cop isn't finished. "Porter sure kept you two on the down low. Guess that makes sense, considering."

Viking Cop plows forward. "Look, with all the activity on the west side...When the call came in—you know, these things can go south in a hurry—we just wanted to make sure everything was copacetic over here."

"It's not. We're being harassed. Someone's knocking on the doors, the windows. For hours now."

Bald Cop is dismissive. "Kids probably."

"That's what we thought. Then, the last one, my wife saw the guy's hand banging on the window."

"Black or white?"

"I don't know. But it was an adult. Definitely an adult. Other than that, I...I don't know."

"Any problems with the neighbors? Run-ins with anyone on the block?"

"No. Nothing."

"We get along with everybody. That we know of."

Bald Cop is using his flashlight to spotlight the address. "D'ya make sure Porter got his pound of flesh?"

"Thanks, Keith, I got this."

Bald Cop nods and heads back to his car. He pauses briefly to illuminate the "For Sale" sign. "Gettin' outta Dodge. Smart move."

"Like I said, we just want to get on with our lives."

Viking Cop watches as his colleague gets into his car and pulls away. He turns back to the Wards. "I tell you what, I'll take a look around. Drive through the alley. Check things out for you."

"Thank you. It's probably no big deal. We just didn't know what else to do."

The cop turns to go, then stops. "That was really a bad scene, how that all went down. What I'm trying to say is—I'm very sorry for your loss."

Willow can't hide her bitterness. "We didn't lose her. She's not going to turn up in the lost and found somewhere."

"Willow, this isn't the time..."

"In all fairness, ma'am, the officers thought they were walking into a bad situation."

Willow, her voice drenched in sarcasm, quotes from the official report: "They were operating on their best understanding of the situation at the time."

"Ma'am, like your husband said—"

"You know what her best understanding of the situation is? She doesn't have one. She's dead."

"This is not the time or the place—"

"She was sixteen. She panicked. For God's sake, all she had was a learner's permit."

"Ma'am, I understand—"

"How could anyone be afraid of D? Big, goofy, funny, soft-hearted D?" Willow finally runs out of steam. Her voice is reduced to a whisper. "She was coming home. She would have. I know it."

"Look, don't beat yourselves up. Black kids run away from Black parents too. Happens all the time."

Willow's face is a frozen mask of fury. "Please. Leave."

Viking cop nods, then turns and heads back to his car. Joel pats his wife reassuringly on the arm and then follows the police officer down the front walk. "Can you tell me what's happening on the west side?"

The cop reaches his car and stops. His manner has turned officious. "Everything's under control, sir. Nothing to be concerned about."

Joel turns to look at the inferno illuminating the west side. Clearly, everything is not under control. The policeman gets into the patrol car. He reaches through the open window to hand Joel a business card before pulling away. "Call the precinct if you have any more problems."

J oel and Willow stand at the kitchen window and watch the patrol car drive through the alley. The driver slows briefly to drag a spotlight beam along the side of the rail embankment before speeding up and disappearing into the darkness.

Willow is seething. "D was our daughter. Period."

"Don't try that moral one-upmanship on me. You didn't even want to go through with the adoption, remember?"

"That was a long time ago. I'd led a pretty sheltered life up till then. I'm a different person now. Have been for a long, long time. You, of all people, should know that."

"What was your precious family going to think? That's all you cared about." Mimicking: "'Boy, that kid's got quite the suntan, huh?'"

"It was a stupid thing to say. My father didn't mean any—"

"Then, all of a sudden, you—who never even actually met a real Black person until you went to college—are the world expert on race."

"That's not fair..."

"She was a prop. Raising an abandoned Black child made you relevant. How many diversity initiatives did you initiate? Huh? How many committees did you chair?"

"Just stop. We both wanted a newborn, an infant..."

"Scarce commodity in those days, that's for sure."

"She was a child in need of a home. It didn't matter to me if she was Black, brown, white, or...or polka dot."

They stand in silence, staring out the window at nothing in particular. Joel decides to lower the temperature. "Yeah, polka dot. Now that would have got people talking. Right?"

Willow is not finished. "And yes, once we had D, once it really hit home to me how things were..."

He raises his hands in a gesture of appeasement. "Look, I'm sorry. We don't need to re-litigate all this—"

"Yes, I joined every civil rights organization under the sun. Yes, I signed every petition. Yes, I marched in every protest. Yes, I tutored Black students. Yes, I spearheaded every initiative with the word diversity in its name. But D was never a prop. Never. She was my child. My baby." Her voice begins to break. "Our baby..."

"I know. I know. I'm sorry..."

There's no stopping her now. "People change. I changed. And yes, I went from clueless to committed to the cause in a heartbeat." She turns on him, fierce. "Well, goddammit! Good for me! Goddamn good for me! I make no apologies."

Her hands are shaking as she fills a glass with water. She coaxes a pill out of a plastic pill bottle and puts it in her mouth. She washes it down with a sip of water. "And I thought we were done talking about my dad."

"Look, I'm sorry. I didn't mean to—"

"Stop apologizing all the..." The plastic pill bottle slips from her fingers as she's putting the cap back on. They both watch as the tiny canister rolls in a wide arc across the entire length of the kitchen floor before suddenly tacking to the right and scooting underneath the refrigerator.

Joel grabs the flashlight off the counter and drops to his hands and knees. "Every damn time..."

He shines the light under the fridge and pokes his fingers underneath until the bottle comes rolling out. He grabs it and reaches up to set it on the counter.

Willow is still staring at the spot where the pill bottle rolled under the fridge. "Just one more household microaggression."

"What?"

"That's what D called them: household microaggressions." One corner of her mouth lifts in advance of a knowing smile. "They only happen to us, apparently."

"What? Parents?"

She looks at him, smiling now, without mirth. "White people."

"She didn't..."

There is a loud knock at the front door.

———

J oel uses the countertop to leverage himself to his feet. He gestures urgently to Willow. "C'mon! You need to watch the windows!"

She trails behind as he runs through the house to the front door. He jabs his finger at her as he grips the doorknob. "Watch the windows, dammit!"

Joel bolts through the front door and launches himself off the porch. He sticks the landing this time and charges across the lawn. He stops at the corner and looks around. Nothing. No one. "Son of a bitch! Goddamn son of a bitch!"

He pokes the flashlight beam into the darkness as he jogs along the street side of the house on his way back to the alley. There's no one there. He runs into the alley and rakes the beam of light up and down the embankment. Nothing but weeds and rotting railroad ties.

His shoes crunch gravel as he crosses the alley to check the back gate. It's secured on the inside. He rotates on his heels, doing a full 360 to check his surroundings. The fires on the west side are casting an ethereal glow on the underside of the rail overpass. Nearby houses are dark and desolate. There's no sign of movement on any of the intersecting streets.

Willow is standing in the living room when he comes back inside. She looks at him expectantly. He stares back at her. "What did you see out the window?"

She seems puzzled by the question. "Nothing."

"You must have seen something." He gestures to the windows in the front. "They'd have to have gone right past the fucking window."

"I didn't see anything."

He's angry now, insistent. "How did you not see them? They had to go right past you."

"Maybe they went the other way. Maybe you missed them."

He stares at her, eyes open wide, his tone sarcastic. "Did you see me? The crazy guy running around with a flashlight?"

Willow is cowed by his anger. "No, I didn't. See you."

He stares at her in astonishment. "What do you mean, no?"

"I thought you must have gone around the other way. Through the yard, maybe."

"Are you fucking blind?"

"Don't talk to me like that. How dare you talk to me like that!"

"Then quit acting like a fucking idiot."

She turns away from him, rigid with anger. He seems as if he's going to say something more. Maybe apologize. Instead, he leaves the room and stomps down the basement stairs.

Joel emerges from the basement a few minutes later with a long black crowbar. Willow is no longer in the living room, so he moves to the dining room and peers into the kitchen. Willow is pouring herself a glass of wine. "You know you shouldn't...With your meds..."

She slams the bottle down hard on the table. "Fuck off."

He makes a dismissive gesture. "Suit yourself." He turns and goes into the living room.

———

J oel has turned off all the lights in the house and stationed himself by the front door with the crowbar. Willow is on the couch. They are two murky shapes in a room dimly illuminated by the streetlight outside.

"I still can't figure out how they're doing it. How do they get away so fast?" He allows for the faintest glimmer of hope. "Maybe it's over. I mean, how much time and energy can someone devote to harassing a couple of complete strangers?"

Willow gets up from the couch and stands with her arms folded in front of her. "I don't know. I don't care. I just want to go. I can have Jacob meet us somewhere. We can come back in the morning."

"They could vandalize the house." He turns to Willow to reinforce his point, but she silences him with an upraised hand. "What?"

She looks around the room in wonder, as if seeing it for the first time. "It's the house. It has to be. The house wants us gone."

Joel is too astonished to even be angry. "Where is all this coming from? Like you said, we've completely renovated every piece of this house. With our own hands. You, me...and D. It's our house."

"D is gone. And we don't belong here. Not anymore. Maybe we never belonged here. Maybe it only worked because she was here. And now..."

He moves across the room to her. "Sweetheart, everything's fine. It's going to be okay. We're both going a little bit nuts. Ever since...Look, I'm sorry if I got a little out of line there."

He realizes she is staring at the iron bar in his hand. "What? You think I'd...?" He leans the crowbar against the table with a dull metallic thump, inadvertently destabilizing the stack of photo albums. He quickly drops to one knee to retrieve one that has fallen to the floor while she struggles to corral the rest.

The cellphone rings on the table beside her. She sees who it is and immediately puts it on speaker. "Jacob?"

Jacob can barely be heard over the shriek of sirens and distant shouts. "Willow? Thank God. Look, I've been pulled over. I'll need you to..." He starts speaking to someone else. "I'm just making a quick call. I'll be right with you."

"Jacob, what's—?"

"If I don't get there in time, just remember, it's nothing personal. It's not about you. It just..." He seems to be at a loss for words. "It just is what it is."

"What? What are you talking about?"

Jacob doesn't respond. They hear another man's voice nearby, loud, demanding. "Let me see your hands!"

Jacob sounds frightened. "It's my cell. Just my cell."

There is the sound of the phone tumbling. A thud. Scrambling, grunting, rustling noises. Jacob sounds out of breath. "Just dropped my..."

There is the creak of a car door hinge. Panicked, angry voices. "Hands! Let me see your fucking hands!"

Willow grabs the phone from the table. "Jacob? Jacob?"

The phone goes dead. Willow hits redial, but it goes immediately to Jacob's voicemail. She hangs up and turns to Joel. She's frantic. "We need to do something. We need to call someone—"

There is a powerful knock on the front door. Then another, even louder. And another, a resounding blow. It sounds as if someone is trying to break the door down. Joel is momentarily taken aback by the ferocity of the assault but quickly recovers and grabs the crowbar.

"Son of a bitch!" He moves to the door, shouting to Willow over his shoulder. "Lock the door behind me! The deadbolt!"

<hr>

J oel flings the door open and rushes out onto the porch. A quick scan reveals that the lawn and the street out front are clear. He leaps off the porch and scrambles over to the side of the house. He directs the beam of the flashlight to the side door, the fence gate, the darkened windows of the house next door, their own pitch-dark house. There's no one there. No one! Nothing!

He goes through the gate and into the yard, scanning his surroundings with the flashlight beam as he goes: the concrete pad where the new garage was supposed to go, the refinished deck, the raised planter boxes, the carefully tended islands of grass bordered by garden-store landscape rocks.

He exits the back gate and moves urgently through the alley. It's deserted. He stands there for a moment, perplexed, then stuffs the flashlight into his pocket and begins scaling the side of the rail embankment. He jams the iron bar repeatedly into the turf to anchor himself as he pulls himself up the slope to the very top.

When Joel reaches the crest of the embankment, he feels as if he's mounted the parapet of a walled city. The vista to the west reveals a city under siege, all smoke and flames and flashing emergency lights. Behind him, to the east, are the dark, deserted streets of his own neighborhood.

Looking to the south, the cold iron in his grip, sends a chill through his arms and into his shoulders as he recalls the embattled streets of his childhood.

In those days, it was a broad avenue that served as the wall, the de facto barrier separating mutually hostile Black and white neighborhoods. Joel was not an aggressive kid by any means, but he got into countless fights. It was a fact of life. You got your ass kicked for being white on the wrong side of the avenue. And God help you if you were Black on the side he lived on. And that doesn't even take into account the other white kids who wanted a piece of him, driven by the need to take out their frustrations on somebody, anybody, after finding themselves an embattled minority in an increasingly Black city.

Nights were the worst. Residents of both races locked themselves in their homes while their children roamed the streets like adolescent gladiators. It was rough. But his family was white, and they had options. They could leave. And they did.

All in all, he thinks, *it was an invaluable life lesson learned young. There are good white people and white people who suck. There are good Black people and Black people who suck. There are white people who work hard and make it and some who are too damned lazy, or stupid, or whatever, and don't. There are Black people who work hard and make it and some who don't. So fucking be it. Was it so terrible that he was determined to make sure his own daughter was one of the good ones?*

Joel turns and starts back down the embankment. He's tempted to toss away the crowbar, but then, gazing out at the bleak, empty streets, he decides to keep it.

W illow engages the deadbolt and stands there, shoulder to the door, as if the effort required to turn that small brass knob has left her physically drained. She slumps down on the steps leading upstairs. She remembers that time in sixth grade. The science fair. Something she hasn't thought about in years. Not since D. Not since long before D.

She was on an outing with her classmates that took them from their suburban school district to the civic center downtown. After a perfunctory tour of the exhibits, she found a gaggle of her friends leaning over a concrete wall overlooking an alley at the back of the multi-level parking structure. They were throwing nickels and dimes to a bunch of neighborhood Black kids in the alley below, laughing gleefully as the children scrambled for the coins.

They were yelling something at the kids she'd never heard before. It was a word so ugly sounding she instinctively knew it was wrong. That harsh N, the I, the G... Everything about that word was somehow coarse and jagged. And the gleeful abandon of her friends hurling it at those little kids along with the coins was jarring but somehow also thrilling.

She fished around in her little string purse for some spare-change and joined her friends at the ledge. She hurled a handful of coins that spattered across the pavement like pebbles across the surface of a still pond. Her friends jeered as the little Black boys jostled each other in their eagerness to scoop them up. Willow suddenly felt flushed with shame.

She turned and walked back to the bus by herself. She sat there, brooding in silence, until the rest of her classmates swaggered onboard for the long ride home. She told herself she was never going to think about it again. *Thank God I never told Joel that story.*

Willow takes out her phone. She reads the number off the cop's business card and dials, but there's no service. She pockets the phone, rises, and turns to go up the steps. She can't do it. Her nerves, scraped raw by the ongoing harassment, are no match for the dark void at the top of the stairs.

She goes to the coffee table and grabs as many of the photo albums as she can comfortably carry. She returns to the staircase and, pressing the albums to her chest like an infant, mounts the steps with more confidence.

Joel can feel the tremors from an approaching train as he stands on the front walk. He's run out of places to look, so he stuffs the flashlight into his pocket and wearily mounts the porch steps. He goes to open the front door, but it's locked. He tries the key but realizes the deadbolt is on. *Wouldn't you know it? This would be the one damn time she gets it right.*

He starts to press the doorbell but remembers it's not working and knocks on the door instead. There's no answer. He leans in close to the door. "Will? Are you there?" Nothing. He steps back and looks up. There are no lights on upstairs. The house looks like it could be abandoned.

Joel leaps off the porch and hurries around to the side door. That door is locked as well, and chained from the inside. He raps angrily on the solid wood with the curved end of the crowbar. "Willow, what the fuck? Let me in the goddamn house!" There's nothing. No response.

The agitation from the approaching train has grown stronger by the time he moves to the kitchen window. He taps on the glass with his knuckles, but the window is already vibrating so violently from the surrounding turmoil that he is afraid it will break. He leans close to look through the window and stumbles back in panic when he finds himself staring into the eyes of a stranger. "What the...?!"

He moves cautiously back to the window for another look. All he can see inside the house is a black void, and he realizes he must have been startled by his own reflection.

Joel trots back around to the front door and knocks again. There's still no response. The train must be passing directly behind the house now, and the once stolid brick walls and limestone sills appear to shimmy as the hundreds of tons of steel and freight moving across the embankment agitate the structure like tiny aftershocks. Angry now, he ignores the growing tumult and steps forward to pound on the door with his fist. Then he kicks it, again and again, but the stout wood portal is impervious to his blows.

The roar of the train is building to a crescendo as Joel cuts across the lawn toward the street side of the house. He stops in confusion when he finds himself wading through deep, matted grass. He looks around to find his well-manicured lawn completely overtaken by a dense, unruly tangle of weeds and turf. The *"For Sale"* sign is nearly obscured by the sudden growth.

The concussive turbulence from the passing train is causing the entire house to rock. The wood shutters framing the windows are flapping rhythmically against the brick, and the bolts securing drainpipes to their metal brackets are working themselves loose. As the tumult builds in intensity, the house sheds several tiles that slide down the pitched roof and get hung up in the rain gutter. The entire structure is now lurching from side to side, as if trying to free itself from the foundation.

This must be the goddamn train from hell, Joel thinks as he turns the corner of the house. Then, he stops and stares at the rail embankment in astonishment. There is no train. The massive berm, silhouetted against the glowing sky to the west, is dark and silent. He stands there frozen as the ferment that seems to have possessed the house slowly tapers off until everything is still.

Before he can process this new development, Joel spots a single headlight emerging from beneath the rail underpass. It's a police cruiser. Relieved, Joel walks into the street and flags down the approaching car. The rotating blue beacon atop the car begins to flash as it rolls to a stop beneath the streetlight.

Joel is shocked to see that the windshield is a quilted web of crumpled glass. The hood, one headlight, the roof, and both driver-side doors look as if they've been tenderized with baseball bats. Behind the police cruiser, beyond the rail embankment, the west side is a solid curtain of smoke and flames. The door opens with a protesting creak of steel hinges, and a cop climbs out. A Black cop. Joel takes a hesitant step toward him.

"I am so glad to see you..."

The cop unholsters his gun, braces both arms atop the open door, and takes aim at Joel. "Stop right there."

Joel, remembering the crowbar in his hand, raises both arms at his sides. The cop moves from behind the car door and approaches him, gun at the ready. The cop is a burly guy with the slightly padded physique of a former athlete and what appears to be a permanent scowl.

His uniform shirt pocket is ripped, and the knees of his trousers are stained with asphalt and tiny bits of gravel. As he moves closer, his demeanor is softened somehow by the Carl Weathers' stache covering his upper lip.

"Set it down. Easy."

Joel crouches and sets the crowbar gently down on the ground.

"Get down on your knees." Joel hesitates, and the cop takes a menacing step toward him. "Now! Goddammit!"

Joel kneels in the street, arms out to his sides. "Hey, bro, I'm the homeowner here."

"Don't bro me. My mamma didn't raise no ugly-ass kids like you." He gestures with the gun. "That blood?"

Joel looks at the crowbar and realizes the bottom portion of the shaft is coated with something dark and red, maybe paint, maybe rust, maybe...? "No, oh God no, just rust. Must be rust. Or dirt or something. It's old, really old. Here when we moved in."

The cop holsters the gun and pats Joel down. Finished, he takes a step back and studies his prisoner. "Don't exactly look like Dillinger to me. And you sure as hell ain't Antifa." His gaze moves to the house. "What are you doing out here?"

"I live here. I just..."

"Let me see some I.D."

Joel reaches into his back pocket for his wallet. "Got locked out." He takes out his license and hands it to his interrogator. "Deadbolt's on the front door, so I was going around to the back."

The cop examines the license. "Mister Ward?"

"Yes, sir—officer."

Joel waits expectantly, but the name doesn't seem to mean anything to the cop, who continues to stare at the license. He reads off the address. "Four five two Copley. Why does that ring a bell?"

"We...My daughter...She..."

"That's right: the LeFlore house." He turns to gaze at the house for a moment, and his voice goes cold. "Looks real different now. Almost don't recognize the place." He sighs and shakes his head, as if attempting to erase a bad memory. His voice is grim. "Night just keeps gettin better and better."

He stuffs the license into what remains of his shirt pocket while continuing to study the dark house. "Power out?"

"No. I turned off all the lights. It's...It's hard to explain."

The cop turns his attention back to Joel. "So, explain. Why is the deadbolt on and you're creeping around out here with a Mexican master key?"

"My wife. She locked the deadbolt. Now she's not letting me in."

"Sounds like maybe she's afraid of you."

"Oh no, it's nothing like that. I told her to lock the door."

The cop looks skeptical. "Did you tell her not to unlock the door and let you back in?"

Joel is at a loss. "I...I don't know. I don't know what's going on." He gestures weakly to his knees on the rough pavement. "Can I get up?"

"Go ahead." Joel clambers to his feet. The cop reaches into his pocket to hand Joel his license. "Any reason she'd want to lock you out of the house? Be afraid of you?"

"No, absolutely not. I mean, there's been some—a lot really—stress lately." He is surprised suddenly, by how overcome with emotion he is. His voice is shaking. "We lost our daughter. Our only child. She was...She was killed." He stops himself from going any further.

The cop's tone turns sympathetic. "I'm sorry to hear that. That's gotta be rough, losing a child." He grabs his radio mic clip and presses the call button. "I tell you what, I'm going to—"

The radio emits a chattering stream of static, and he quickly shuts it off. "Every damn thing's going sideways tonight." He gives up on the radio and removes the handcuffs from his belt. "I want you to know, this is for your safety and mine..."

"You're not going to arrest me? This is my house." He gestures to the crowbar. "I'm only out here with that because we're being harassed, my wife and I. We called the police. It's been going on all night. That's why I'm so..." He doesn't have the words and can only manage a flailing arm gesture. "That's probably why my wife..."

The cop glances over his shoulder at the inferno on the west side before turning his attention back to the slightly pathetic, middle-aged guy standing in front of him. He puts the cuffs away. "Give me the flashlight. Mine's..." He looks back at his battered cruiser and sighs. "Out of service."

Joel hands him the flashlight. The cop makes a point of picking up the crowbar before moving toward the house. He stops and uses the crowbar as a pointer: "You stay right there. You hear me?"

Joel nods. The cop crosses the lawn, wades through the now thigh-high grass, and climbs the porch steps. He sets the crowbar down on the cement and goes to press the doorbell.

"Doesn't work." His voice gets very small. "I was supposed to fix it."

The cop knocks on the front door. "Mrs. Ward? Open up, please." He tries the door and finds it locked with the deadbolt. He knocks again. "It's okay, Mrs. Ward, it's the police." There's no response, so he steps off the porch and walks back to where Joel is waiting. "You sure she's there?"

"Positive. There's no way she could have gone anywhere."

"Why won't she come to the door? Any medical issues?"

Joel hesitates before answering. "No, of course not. Nothing that would...Maybe you could try the back door? There's no deadbolt." He reaches into his pocket, and the alarmed cop puts a hand on his gun. Joel freezes. "I was just going to give you a key."

The cop relaxes his grip on the gun. "Go ahead."

Joel pulls out the house key. His hand is trembling. "Back door. That's where I was going."

The cop takes the key and glances briefly at the NPR keychain before pocketing it. He turns and moves along the privacy fence toward the alley, calling over his shoulder. "You got a dog?"

"No. No, sir. Officer, I mean. Our daughter was..." His voice trails off. "Nothing. Never mind."

The cop turns into the alley and opens the back gate to the yard. He stops, stunned by what he sees. "Lord have mercy..."

This is not the same yard Joel has patrolled throughout the evening. The skittering flashlight beam reveals mounds of weathered trash and thickets of overgrown weeds. There is a toppled children's jungle gym in the high grass that could be the mossy ribcage of a long-dead whale.

The cop is forced to pick his way through an obstacle course of garbage, partially buried car tires, and broken concrete to get to the back deck. He crosses the deck but then stops with his closed fist poised to knock on the door.

At least in the front of the house, with the homeowner watching from the street, there was the small comfort of another person being present. But now... Officer Roy Sermon, former marine, twelve-year veteran of the force, is having a moment. He remembers this house. *Oh, dear God me, I remember this house. That was a long time ago,* he reassures himself. *A very long time ago.*

He adjusts his holster, stands rigidly straight, and gives himself a talking to: C'mon now, you're a grown-ass man. Then, he knocks loudly. "Mrs. Ward?" There's no response, and he raps on the door again, harder this time. "Mrs. Ward, this is the police. There's nothing to be afraid of. I just want to make sure you're okay."

Roy turns the key in the lock and goes inside. He hits the light switch by the door, but nothing happens. "Figures." The cop moves through the cramped back hallway and into the kitchen. He stops and uses the flashlight beam as a follow-spot to track a fat roach scurrying across the worn Formica countertop. Then he looks around.

There is no HGTV-inspired farmhouse sink. No stylish blonde-wood open shelving. No stainless-steel appliances. This kitchen is a shabby time capsule from another era. The enormous cast-iron skillet and stockpot on the stove look like they belong in an early 20th century boarding house. And he hasn't seen a refrigerator this old since that TV show about two Iowa picker boys riding around looking for old-timey shit to sell. None of this makes sense, he thinks. That yard, this kitchen—and that white guy out there in the street—are from different planets. Different universes.

The other half of the eat-in kitchen presents a stark contrast. The walls—aside from the colorful, eighteen-inch-tall letters spelling out "Peace. Love. Wine."—are bare. The printed fabric curtains match the sky-blue place mats on the table. The table, sleek, white-painted pine with a butcher block top and four upholstered chairs, is what Roy would expect from the gentrifiers who have colonized the neighborhood in recent years. He can imagine that guy out there on the street sitting down at this table with his coffee and his English muffin in the morning. He turns back to shine the light on the scruffy half of the kitchen. *Now that just don't make no sense.*

Roy keeps moving, and the flashlight beam reveals an adjoining dining room that is packed full with moving boxes. He flips another useless light switch before stepping into the room. The chic brass and crystal chandelier overhead looks like an old-school TV antenna that's been gold-plated and hung upside down. The dining room table has been pushed up against the wall and is stacked high with unassembled moving cartons. The white, glass-door cabinets along the other wall contain nothing but tape and packing materials.

Turning back in the direction of the kitchen, his flashlight beam illuminates the side door to the house and another leading to the basement stairs. He turns back around and follows the darting flashlight beam into the living room. The couch and chairs are Scandinavian-lite, and the glass and chrome coffee table is piled high with what appear to be antique photo albums.

The inquisitive halo of light skims the gallery of large, metal-framed, museum art posters lining the walls. Some of them look vaguely familiar, and he pauses to read the names of the artists. *Yeah, that's Romare Bearden. Right? Harlem, must be,* he thinks. The others—an odd mixture of modern and primitive—are attached to names that mean nothing to him: Jacob Lawrence. Bill Traylor. Martin Puryear.

Losing interest, he directs the light to a side table where it discovers a framed portrait of the mixed-race family that now occupies the house. The parents are white—one of them the man outside with the crowbar. The teenage daughter, already taller than her mother, is Black, with a throwback, cotton candy afro and eyes far too old for her face. The three of them are posed with the stiff, dutiful smiles of a staged professional photo shoot.

After a moment, he senses as much as he hears a low rumble that seems to emanate from somewhere beneath his feet. At first, he thinks it must be a train passing by on the railway berm behind the house. But as the vibration grows stronger, he realizes it's coming from inside the house.

Probably the furnace kicking on in the basement, he thinks. *Awful early in the season to be using the heat.*

Officer Sermon turns to study the staircase. He knows what he has to do: he has to go up those stairs. Again. He does not want to go up those stairs. He does not want to go back into that room. The one at the back of the house. The one in the corner overlooking the street and the rail embankment. The one with the locked door they had to beat down all those years ago when he was a young cop.

He knows he doesn't have a choice. He's a cop. He took an oath. *It's my job to go up those damn stairs.* He decides to go check the basement first.

Willow has locked herself in the upstairs bathroom. The power has gone out, and she's perched on the toilet in the dark. The stack of photo albums occupies her lap like a sleeping cat, and she's using the phone's flashlight app to flip through the top one.

The dense weight of the albums on her lap is calming somehow, and she remembers how she used to sit for hours, slowly turning the pages and studying each photograph. She'd fabricate little stories behind the moment captured in a particular image, inventing names and histories for the long-departed men, women, and children depicted. Over time, she began to insert D into her little dioramas. She'd imagine her daughter, happy, smiling, wrapped in the warm embrace of grandparents, aunts, uncles, cousins, nieces, nephews, and siblings. People who looked like her. People who were Black. Like D.

Sure, they have plenty of pictures of D. With Willow's family. With Joel's family. With friends and colleagues over the years. Their white friends. Their white colleagues. Their white extended families. And their Black child. But, no matter how much she was accepted, no matter how much she was loved, D's visage always provided the answer to the question: Which one does not belong in this picture?

Then, over time, Willow began to insert herself into those old photographs alongside her daughter. She'd fantasize about the two of them firmly embedded in this imagined Black world where race no longer mattered and they were embraced as simply mother and daughter. But she didn't stop there. Having a Black daughter had given her entre and Willow discovered that she enjoyed socializing with the families of D's Black classmates.

Sure, she had to endure some good-natured ribbing about her name and her long blonde mane— "Honey, did you steal that child?" —but she was attracted to the warmth, the bantering, the immediate familiarity bestowed on even the most casual encounter. It was nothing like her family growing up. Her parents and extended family were stiff, formal, secretive. No one touched. No one made small talk with strangers. They didn't even talk that much to each other.

As a child, Willow had mastered the polite, diffident smile. She'd allowed others to take credit for her accomplishments, to nudge her out of the limelight, to silence her. But the same suburban cul-de-sac childhood that had so disarmed Willow had fashioned D into a warrior. D didn't have the option to hang back, to get lost in the crowd, to defer. The irony was, by raising a Black child in a white world, Willow no longer had that option either. If she was going to protect her child, she had to learn to speak up.

Her first tentative efforts were swatted away. The imperious store clerk insisted she was following D around the shop to see if she needed assistance. The clueless teacher assured Willow that D's guffawing white classmates were more than mature enough to deal with the n-word in Ma Rainey's Black Bottom. With practice, she got better, not just more assertive at supporting her daughter, but more effective. And then, with the move into the city, with their exposure to a more diverse community, it became a moot point. Or so she had thought.

By the time she was in her second semester at the charter, D had developed an attitude with her parents. At first, Willow kind of liked this new, sassier D. Her daughter had perfected a stock phrase—delivered with a smirky eye-roll—when Joel said something she determined to be particularly clueless. "That's very white of you, Dad."

Joel was not amused, but Willow laughed along with their daughter. What did he expect? Trying to shame her for giggling over the little Black boys in The Boondocks using the n-word? And the rap music she listened to? Why even go there? That ship sailed a long time ago.

Sometimes, when her husband said something particularly obtuse, she'd roll her eyes and mouth the words to D herself, "That's so white of you." It became a little shared joke between them. Until it wasn't. Until the gibe was directed at her and she got her feelings hurt.

And just what was so 'positively grotesque' about offering to throw my own daughter a natural hair party?— she wonders. She'd helped D with her hair since she was a child. She'd read all the articles about Black hair in Good Housekeeping and watched a slew of TikTok and YouTube videos. *I was trying. Trying so hard. I didn't deserve to be seated in the Clueless White People section.*

Willow closes the photo album and sets it down on the floor. She gazes absently at the next album, brushing her fingertips across the pebbled surface as she prepares to open it. Then, she freezes and brings the smartphone light in close to examine the cover. By all appearances, it's just one more standard, albeit badly scuffed and seriously old, LeFlore family photo album. But she knows from painful experience that this one is different. This is the Photoshop version D created for that school project.

How in God's name...? Joel told me he got rid of...

Her hands clench as she relives the humiliating visit from the school social worker. "How is your daughter's home life? Is there something we should know about? Where is all the anger coming from? Why did she stop playing sports? Do you know where she might have gotten the idea to do something like this? Why do you call her D and not her given name?"

Willow snorts at that particular memory. She always liked the name D. Sort of hip. Like a rapper. In any case, it was better than the name Joel originally talked her into: Diamond. Their "diamond in the rough." *What in God's name were we thinking?*

All of that pales in comparison to what happened next, after that humorless bureaucrat left and all-out war erupted between D and her father. Joel lectured their daughter about her ingratitude. How they'd rescued her from a probable life of poverty and hopelessness. How they'd sent her to the best schools, summer camps, sports camps, school trips... "And this is how you repay us?"

Willow struggled to play referee, but Joel went off the deep end when D screamed in his face that her adoption by white parents was "nothing more than the logical continuation to slavery. It's all about control. It's just the latest iteration of the Black/white power dynamic."

Willow, in spite of everything, couldn't help but be impressed by the increased sophistication of her daughter's vocabulary since enrolling in the charter. Joel, mouth agape, was speechless. D held her ground. "I'm simply taking my power back. Deal with it." For a moment, Willow had feared there would be a physical confrontation.

Afterward, Joel tried to laugh it off. "Two things you should never do," he grinned, "Fight a land war in Asia, or argue with a teenage girl."

Willow couldn't really blame her husband for losing it after some of the hurtful things his daughter had said to him, but she reminded him that they needed to be the adults in the room. Joel continued to downplay the rift with their daughter. He called their screaming match "The

Thrilla in Manila. Used my patented, parental rope-a-dope to wear her down. Now she's up in her room contemplating the error of her ways."

Willow didn't find it the least bit funny. Joel had a habit of saying boneheaded things like that, as if his early years in the city gave him license to disregard any sort of filter when it came to race. His "Look at all the popo here at the MoMo" comment to D and her Black friends, while escorting them through security at the art museum, marked the end to his brief stint as a chaperone on school trips and the beginning of the long downward slope in his relationship with his daughter.

Willow opens the heavy faux-leather cover of D's facsimile photo album and starts to turn the pages. These are not the family snapshots that have so comforted her. The tiny photo corners no longer grip images of family barbeques and smiling children. Instead, each Photoshopped image has become a mug shot depicting a Black man, woman, or child. Each of them is staring directly into the camera. Frightened. Angry. Sullen. Smiling. Bashful. Grinning. Bored. Hopeful. Hopeless. Defiant.

Many of the black and white images seem to be contemporary; others could be from previous decades. Still others, manipulated to look faded and sepia-toned, appear to go all the way back to the late 19th century. Willow can't resist a wry smile. All those summer computer camps really paid off.

She stops turning the pages. She doesn't want to see the pages where D had Photoshopped images of her Black classmates and other people of color—her teachers, the mayor, famous athletes and celebrities—into mug shots as well. And she really does not want to see the final, searing mugshot that D composed using her own image, the one of

her daughter staring into the camera with such frighten-
ing intensity she is nearly unrecognizable.

Her face is the embodiment of fury. Her eyes, icy with
rage, reveal not even the slightest glint of understanding
or forgiveness. In that Photoshopped mugshot, created on her daughter's laptop, in that room upstairs, D
looked—there's no other way to describe it—possessed.
Willow hurls the book to the floor. Then she leans down
to shine the light on the battered album, half hoping it
was all an illusion. It's not.

Officer Roy Sermon experiences an overpowering
sense of dread as he descends the basement steps.
He's back in the turret of an armored Humvee, waiting to
be blown to kingdom come by an IED. The body armor,
the welded steel plate, the weapons, the ammo belts, the
electronics, all seem woefully inadequate as you watch
the vehicle ahead of you disintegrate in a greasy, plumed
inferno. Even more disturbing is your inability to separate
the soaring whirligigs of metal and tubing from the torn
limbs and hunks of human flesh that were your friends.

There are no IEDs in the basement, just standing water and murk. The furnace is gone, lost to scrappers
years before, so Roy searches for another explanation for
the growing turbulence rocking the house. He trudges
through the crusted sludge covering the concrete floor
like a deep-sea diver in the sunless depths of the ocean.
The air around him is charged with a dark energy that
smothers the flashlight beam until it is barely capable of
penetrating the gloom.

The walls, the pillars, the ceiling beams, all pulse with an inner life force. There are ominous mounds of rubble that seem to press in on him whenever he shifts his gaze away. Each time he swivels back to shine the light on them, the malevolent shapes transform themselves into harmless heaps of cardboard boxes and clutter.

The low rumble continues to grow in intensity, and Roy is able to trace its source to the back wall of the basement, the one facing the rail embankment. The clamor grows louder as he approaches, and the wall begins to quiver. He crinkles his nose at the stink—gamey and stale—and so dense he has to lean into it to move forward. He goes to press his palm against the damp concrete but pulls back in disgust when it turns out to have the consistency of raw meat.

The whole basement is rocking now, and Roy realizes that, somehow, there is a tunnel on the other side of the wall and a freight train is hurtling right at him. He backpedals with all the dignity of a Kevlar-vested dancing bear until he strikes the metal post behind him. The brain-pounding turbulence has reached a crescendo, and Roy—covering his ears to block out the racket—ducks instinctively as the speeding behemoth hits the opposite wall. Nothing happens. Roy straightens up and shines the beam of the flashlight on the wall. It is inert concrete.

Exiting the basement, Roy enters the eat-in kitchen. As he moves past the table, the polished wood floor beneath his feet suddenly tilts, first to one side, then the other. He flails his arms like a tight-rope walker to steady himself, but then, the entire room becomes the revolving cylinder in a funhouse and cantilevers sharply to the left. Roy loses his balance and slams shoulder-first into the wall. He turns just in time to see the table sliding toward him and drops the flashlight in order to catch it with both hands, plunging the room into darkness.

The room levels and stabilizes with a flabby thump, allowing Roy to fish around on the floor for the flashlight. He turns it on and goes to push the table back into the center of the room. But it's not the same table. The sleek version that was there moments before has been transformed into a thick-legged garage sale find, chipped and scarred from hard use. The chairs are now a mismatched assortment of ladder-backs with sagging cane seats.

He shoves the table back into place and shines the light around the room. The flashlight beam reveals faded portraits on the wall of a blue-eyed Jesus, Martin Luther King, Jr., and John F. Kennedy. The floor beneath his feet is covered in cheap linoleum, and the ruffled, floral pattern curtains remind him of the house where he grew up. There's a wall calendar hanging from a nail on the opposite wall, issued by the Watkins Family Funeral Home. The date printed in the space between the paper calendar grid and the illustration of several angelic Black children is April 1971.

Roy pivots and the flashlight beam reveals the adjoining dining room with its collection of moving boxes. Before he can take another step, the kitchen begins to gyrate like a berserk lunar training module, then cantilevers sharply toward the dining room. Roy breaks into a downhill trot in order to stay on his feet, and his momentum carries him into the plaster wall just to the side of the doorway. He grabs the doorframe and holds onto it as the kitchen lurches drunkenly for several seconds before gradually returning to its original perspective.

Roy takes a moment to catch his breath. When he shines the flashlight around the dining room; the boxes are gone, along with the table, the cabinets, and the chandelier. He instinctively flips the useless light switch before stepping into the room and nearly tripping over a mattress on the floor. As he steadies himself, the flashlight beam spotlights several syringes, and he moves forward more carefully.

The version of the room that has materialized is being used as a crash pad and is crammed with a grungy mish-mash of sleeping bags, mattresses, trash bags stuffed with belongings, and squalid heaps of pizza boxes and fast-food containers. There is a La-Z-Boy recliner in the corner that has collapsed so far in on itself it could have been dropped from an airplane.

By the time Roy reaches the living room, the mysterious turbulence is ratcheting up again. He moves cautiously into the room, testing each step in advance like a man venturing onto an icy pond. The living room looks just as it did before he went into the basement, but the couch and table legs are tap-dancing on the wood floor now. And the pictures on the wall are rattling violently against the plaster.

"Hello? Mrs. Ward? Anybody? Is there anybody here?" Roy stands quietly, listening for a response, for any sign of life, then calls into the void again. "It's the police. You got nothing to be afraid of. Hello?" There's still no answer.

The walls are convulsed by a series of violent spasms, and Roy flinches instinctively as one of the hooks holding up the large Martin Puryear poster gives way. The framed picture scrapes across the plaster before coming to rest at a drunken angle on the wall.

He takes one more look around the room with the flash-light, and the floating halo of light rediscovers the framed family portrait. But the teenage girl is alone in the frame now. Puzzled, he scans the surrounding area to make sure there aren't two separate family photos.

Convinced it's the same picture he saw earlier, he snatches it off the table for a closer look. The images of the white
parents have faded away, leaving only pale, ashen auras
beside the girl to mark their previous existence. Their Black
daughter looks uncomfortable in the awkward space of
the near-empty frame. She's no longer even pretending to
smile.

He sets the picture back on the table. It's time to go
upstairs. Then, he realizes who the girl is and turns the
flashlight back on the photo. *Goddamn, been so many I
didn't even recognize the name. That's Diamond Ward, God
rest her soul. That's the girl got herself shot trying to run over
a cop.*

He turns reluctantly back to the stairs. This house sure
as hell got it in for Black folks.

T he phone light illuminates the bathroom with the
     muted glow of a child's nightlight as Willow stacks
the photo albums on the floor. Growing up in the suburbs,
sports had been D's salvation. She slotted right into it.
That was the perception. She was Black. She was large
for her age. She was supposed to be an athlete. Not that
it was a bad thing. Not at first. She didn't have to argue
with coaches the way she did with teachers about lowered
expectations.

She dealt with her size. Accepted it. It was not so terrible
to tower over other kids when you were dunking on them,
or delivering a hip-check, or scoring a goal. Her white
teammates started calling her Big D, Double D, D-Lite. She
made the traveling squads. She won trophies. She even

started to get letters from colleges. Mostly small private colleges, but still.

Things were different once they moved into the city. At Triumph Academy, she was no longer that one big Black kid in a sea of whiteness. She made Black friends who weren't athletes. She even discovered her inner Black nerd. But it was not as if she was going to disappear, to try to blend in. No, just the opposite. She found her Blackness. On steroids. Almost immediately after they moved into the house, she started to grow the most voluminous afro possible, emphasizing her height to the fullest. She wanted to be big. She wanted to be that scary Black person. She wasn't going to apologize to the world for being tall. For being Black. For being angry.

It was the anger that baffled Willow. At one point she wondered if her daughter might be gay. *Queer is the proper term, I guess. Maybe that would explain all the inner turmoil? The unfathomable rage? The disengagement from her parents?*

She quickly realized it was just wishful thinking on her part; a way to justify D's struggles and her own inability to help. It was a way for Willow to be somehow relevant in her daughter's life. She could never be Black or really know what it's like to be Black. But theoretically at least, she could be gay. Queer. Bisexual maybe. Or transgender. LGBTQIA, right? Questioning? Intersex? Asexual? She could fight that battle, enlist in that army, be eligible for that fight. She could be on the front lines, not somewhere in the rear, cheering from a safe distance and making coffee for the troops.

Then, the thunderclap: D quit. She just gave it up. Walked away. No more sports. No more dreams of college scholarships, the WNBA, the Olympics. She was going to be an activist. She was going to be a lawyer. She was going to change the world. She talked endlessly about reparations. About dismantling white privilege. About justice. About injustice. About redress.

And she brooked no dissent from teachers, friends, or her parents; the subject of race was not open for discussion. Willow chalked it up to a rare contrarian adolescent stage of development not found in the parenting manuals and backed off. But Joel wanted to debate. He was determined to make her understand there were two sides to every argument. But D wasn't having it. There were times Willow feared that Joel and their daughter were going to come to blows.

In between the storms, she was a silent, glowering presence in the house. She holed up in the room upstairs when she wasn't at school. Willow let her be. Decided to give her time. She even convinced Joel to back off. Not that it mattered; D was having nothing to do with him by then.

Willow leans her head against the wall, suddenly very tired, and closes her eyes. One night, watching TV, Joel suddenly hit the mute button. He tilted his head toward D's room upstairs. "When do you think she had her 'come to Jesus' moment up there?"

She knew immediately what he was referring to. Both she and Joel had increasingly come to blame that corner room for what was happening to their daughter. But she didn't want to discuss it. Not now. Not with Joel. "When did you have yours? When did you have your 'come to Jesus' moment?"

He settled back into his chair, annoyed with her for deflecting the question onto him. But, to her surprise, he answered. "Every hour of every day. For a lot of years now."

Now, she was interested. "And where did that get you?"

The smile was forced. "It helped me to assemble the irresistible specimen of woke manhood you see before you."

She was not finding him quite so irresistible. She reached for the remote, but he set it down out of her reach. "We can talk about all that later. Right now, we need to talk about that room upstairs. We need to talk about what's happening to our daughter."

And they did. Not in the depth or the detail that would have been required to get them any closer to understanding what was actually going on with their daughter. That was beyond their comprehension. That would have required a lot more courage and insight than either one of them—as beaten down and exhausted as they were—could muster at that moment in time. But they did come to a decision.

The next day while D was at school, they moved her things out of that awful room and into Willow's home office down the hall. The office walls were covered with a colorful mosaic of African art and civil rights posters, as well as numerous certificates and plaques for her volunteer work with the NAACP. Willow even picked up some calming lavender oil from a Black boutique downtown. She thought the space would comfort D. Fat chance.

Willow wakes with a start and realizes she must have nodded off to sleep. The house is deathly silent, and she wonders if she might still be dreaming. She senses a presence in the room with her and turns on the phone light to find five-year-old D sitting across from her with her back against the door. She's playing with her black T-Rex, trotting it across the bathroom floor and roaring. "ROAR! ROAR!"

Willow knows it's a dream, but she doesn't care. She'll take what she can get. "The T-Rex didn't roar like a lion, sweetie."

D looks at her and smiles. The voice that emerges from her lips is that of the teenage D, not the five-year-old speaking. "No. They produced closed-mouth vocalizations. Maybe a growl, probably more like a honk or a chirp." She thrusts the black T-Rex toward her mom. "But this is a black T-Rex, mom! ROAR! ROAR! ROAR!"

Willow can't help but smile at the plastic toy being shaken in front of her face. "It doesn't matter what color it is, sweetie, it's still a T-Rex."

D's childish smile mirrors her mom's. She presses the toy right up to the tip of her mother's nose. Her voice is suddenly that of the five-year-old. "Mommy, that is so white of you..."

There is an ear-shattering blast, and the room shudders violently, as if every exterior door and window in the house has been blown out at the same instant. The phone light goes out, and Willow can't see her own hand in front of her face in the void that engulfs her.

She remains completely still, listening, but the only sounds now are the creaks and groans of timbers as the house settles. She can't make out D's form in the darkness, but she can sense a presence there. She whispers, "D? Sweetheart?" She can feel the warmth of tears rolling down her cheeks. "Can I hug you? Please?"

There's no answer. She taps the phone app and shines the light on the door. D is gone.

Willow tries to open the door, but it won't budge. It's not locked but seems jammed somehow. She uses the flashlight on her phone to examine it and discovers that the gap between the door and the doorframe has completely disappeared. It's as if the door has swollen in size to completely fill the frame.

She is about to pound on the door when she hears something. She puts her ear to the door and listens. She can hear footsteps. There's someone in the house, but she hasn't heard Joel come back inside. She shoves herself away from the door so fast she jams her ribs into the hard edge of the toilet bowl. She yelps in pain but continues to scoot backward on her ass until she is crammed into the corner between the wall and the toilet. Remembering the phone, she grabs it and sets it to silent.

Whoever it is—whatever it is—is coming closer. Every bit of chrome and glass in the bathroom is rattling with each footfall, and she realizes the intruder is far too big to be a person. The spring-loaded gait, the thudding tread, is that of the beast, the T-Rex of her nightmares. The creature moves steadily closer, and she can hear the sounds of splintering wood as giant claws gouge the floorboards with each step.

The ground beneath her begins to tremble as the creature draws close. Willow clasps her legs tightly to her chest, head pressed hard against her knees, a child willing away the danger with tightly closed eyes.

J oel leans against the patrol car and watches the luminous curtain of smoke that has descended over the west side. He's not used to being out on the street this late at night, and it makes him nervous. The neighborhood is fine during the day, but at night things get a little dicey as boisterous groups of young Blacks from surrounding neighborhoods make their way to and from the nearby business strip.

Joel spent much of his youth and young adulthood tensing up at the sight of Black men—particularly groups of young Black men—approaching on the street at night. *And why not?* He thinks. He's read Black authors who, scarred by the incidents of their youth, describe their own wariness at the sight of young Black men approaching them on the street at night. *Why is it so terrible for him to feel that way?*

D and Willow were always going on and on about white privilege. *Where the hell was my white privilege?*— He wonders—*when I worked my way through college humping freight on loading docks? I'd probably have a Ph.D. like Willow if I'd grown up in those suburbs, went to those schools, had private tutors for the SAT. Hell, I didn't know from the SAT when I was in high school. Worked for every damn thing I got. And where was my goddamn white privilege just now when I had a Black cop pointing a gun at me? In front of my own damn house?*

It's starting to hit him: A cop pointed a gun at him. A Black cop. It's not like he hasn't had guns pointed at him before—among other things—when he was young. Not so far from here even. But that was a long time ago. That was another lifetime. Another life. He's moved on from all that. *Hasn't he?*

He turns his attention back to the house and watches the bright halo from the police officer's flashlight drift through the ground floor. Then, as the shimmering disc skims across the window blinds in the living room, he takes out his phone. He tries to call Willow but he doesn't have any service. He thrusts the phone back into his pocket and starts across the lawn toward the front door.

Joel stops when he realizes the "For Sale" sign is gone. At first, he thinks it's been engulfed in the mysterious growth that has colonized the lawn and paws through the tall grass looking for it. It's not there and, by the time he gives up on his fruitless search, there's no longer any sign of the cop's flashlight inside the house. The first floor has gone completely dark.

Joel picks up the crowbar from the porch but quickly drops it with an involuntary shudder. *What is it about tonight? This fucking house?* He can't stop staring at the iron bar. It was the summer following the riots, and they had moved back into the city after his father's death. He was sixteen, and it was his first real job, at a warehouse downtown. The crew was pretty evenly split between Black and white and the racial tension was at a constant low boil. Joel was a kid and everyone else was in their twenties. He quickly realized he was in way over his head and kept mostly to himself.

Lawrence—Black, wide as a door, a man whose entire face joined the party when he smiled—took pity on the pudgy white kid and took him under his wing. Lawrence worked nights stocking shelves at a pharmacy before coming in to his day job at the warehouse. His eyes were permanently bloodshot, and his wise-cracking exuberance didn't always camouflage a chronic low-level state of exhaustion. Even so, he was a charismatic force of nature on the warehouse floor, and his favor put the shy white kid off-limits to the constant racial friction. Joel was in thrall of the guy.

Things were pretty chill after that. Joel was ignored by his white co-workers and treated as a sort of mascot or with indifference by most of the Black ones. Until the fight at the punch clock. During a heated argument, Vince, a sullen, blonde toadstool from the north side, called Lawrence the

N-word. They started throwing punches, and the rest of the crew crowded around to urge them on. Vince was getting the worst of it when, knocked back into a workbench, his hand came to rest on a crowbar. He grabbed it and whacked Lawrence several times in the face before the others could stop him.

Joel can still picture Lawrence lying in that pool of blood. He felt helpless and stupid. *Why didn't I do something? What could I have possibly done?* And then he saw Vince, on his hands and knees, scrambling to gather some small objects up from the floor. He was apologizing over and over again. "I'm sorry...I'm so sorry, man...I'm sorry..." Joel was horrified when he realized it was Lawrence's teeth Vince was collecting from the sawdust-covered floorboards.

Then the police showed up. And only made things worse. It was Joel's brutal introduction into the racial topography of the city's warehouses, factories, and working-class bars. But it was only the beginning. He would see and experience worse things in the following years. Much worse. Until he worked, scraped, hustled, and came out the other side. Damaged goods as far as he was concerned. But with a college degree, a career, a wife, and a daughter. And a house. This house.

Joel shakes it off. He picks up the crowbar and climbs the porch steps. Then he stops, confused. Everything looks different from a moment ago. The mailbox is stuffed full of yellowing circulars and catalogs. The beautiful oak door he spent an entire weekend refinishing is a weathered barge of peeling paint and splintered wood. And the antique brass doorknocker he found on the Vintage Hardware site is missing. "Son of a..."

He knocks on the door. "Officer? Officer?" There's no response, so he knocks again with the curved head of the crowbar. "Willow! What the hell's going on?"

He's met with silence, so he drops down into the flowerbed beside the porch and peers through the living room window. He can see the policeman on the stairs, but something is off; the man seems to be moving in slow motion, as if he's underwater. Joel shouts: "Hey! Let me in! Hey!" The cop doesn't respond and continues his painfully slow aquatic crawl up the stairs. Joel pounds on the window, but the glass pane has become rock-solid, like crystal, and muffles his blows.

Joel presses his face against the glass, but everything on the other side of this impenetrable barrier has become hazy, and it's like trying to peer through dirty aquarium water turned to ice. The cop on the stairs is only a vague smudge in the distance now; an ancient bipedal organism trapped in amber. For a brief instant, Joel thinks he can see other nebulous figures moving about with a strange, stilted urgency, but they quickly dissolve into the vaporous slurry on the other side of the window.

He slams the crowbar against the glass in frustration, but it bounces off, breaking his glasses and catching his ear on the rebound and drawing blood. He cries out and cups his bloody ear with his hand. By the time he manages to balance the bent eyeglass frames on his nose, the frozen aquarium water on the other side of the glass has transformed into a churning smog of gas jets, bubble bursts, and gloppy foam. He can no longer see the cop. He can't even see the stairs.

In a panic now, Joel clambers back onto the porch. He strikes the door with his fist, with his foot, with the crowbar, but the blows have no more impact than a child's tiny fists beating on the trunk of a towering redwood. He presses his good ear to the door but hears nothing. He steps back and looks up at the house. He's gazing up at a dark, towering, impenetrable tombstone that used to be his home.

Roy moves cautiously up the staircase to the second floor. The flashlight beam reveals rotted stair treads, so he keeps close to the wall. Then he stops, startled by the sounds of the framed posters on the living room wall crashing to the floor, one after another, in a succession of metallic thumps and crackling eruptions of breaking glass. He stands there, frozen in mid-stride, with one hand pressed to the rough plaster wall that has become warm to the touch, like something alive.

The stairs, the walls, the ceiling, everything, every surface, vibrates with a hallucinatory quiver. All of it is overlaid with an intense rumbling sound, like the throaty growl emanating from deep inside the chest of a hibernating bear. He knows now it's not being generated in the basement. It's the house itself. It's alive. And he is on the inside.

The cop braces himself as a series of increasingly violent convulsions jolts the house. Chunks of the plaster ceiling are shaken loose by the ferment, and the staircase lurches, first to one side, then to the other. Roy, struggling to maintain his balance, thinks ruefully to himself: *Guess the damn thing is waking up. Whatever the hell it is.* Then, there is a loud scraping sound from the living room below, followed by volleys of splintering wood and a demolition derby of colliding furniture and fixtures.

In his mind's eye, he can picture what is happening below. The walls of the living room are moving in from all four sides—like that giant trash compactor in that Star Wars movie—to compress and crush everything in their path. *And I ain't got no direct line to C-3PO.* The racket intensifies as the contents of the room are crammed into a smaller and smaller space and the tangled jumble of objects fractures, collapses, and disintegrates beneath the relentless pressure.

The residue is being churned into a hissing, burbling, percolating muck, and Roy ducks as a series of explosive spumes sends concussive shockwaves up the staircase. Something is steeping in that loathsome demonic brew. The living room, and ultimately the house itself, is mutating, morphing into something completely new. Roy tries to imagine what the rubble of the living room is being transformed into. Another crash pad like the dining room? A museum piece like the kitchen? Or a horror-show like that upstairs bedroom all those years ago? He's not so sure he wants to find out.

After a few moments, the tumult subsides, and the house settles into a grim silence. Roy finds himself wishing he had something with a little more firepower than the regulation 9mm pea shooter in his holster. *A damn assault rifle—hell, maybe a flamethrower—would be nice right about now.* He wouldn't mind having the .44 he took off that gawky teenage boy four, five years back. The kid's hard-ass gangster pose had been badly undercut by the utter guilelessness in the eyes, peeking out from beneath a baseball cap with a visor big enough to hold a damn bird's nest.

Roy cut him a break. Didn't write it up. Gun's been sitting in a tackle box in the garage ever since. He was walking through the Ninth a few months later and his heart sank when he saw that kid again, in the company of a couple of uniforms. Turned out he was there making a report on his mom's car being stolen. Wasn't in school, but he wasn't in the system either. Roy smiles as he remembers giving the startled kid a pound. "My man." Small victories.

Roy peers up at the dark landing. *What about Mrs. Ward? Where is she? Is she in danger? If she is, it's my job to do something about it.* The answers are all upstairs. But he doesn't want to go upstairs. *Not again. Dear God, not again.* Roy takes the next step.

———

Willow is sitting on the toilet seat in the dark, knees drawn up to her chin, arms clasped tightly around her legs. *Thank God the room has finally stopped shaking!*

During the worst of it, she tried to block everything out by imagining the entire house being loaded onto one of those flatbed rail cars and hauled out of the city with her still inside. *Where would I go?—* she wonders— *Back to the suburbs? Back to that sterile world of cul-de-sacs, strip malls, and Buffalo Wild Wings?*

Back to a world without sidewalks? Without corner markets and Black barbershops? Without shabby-chic food co-ops and storefront churches? But also a world without cashiers behind bulletproof Plexiglas dividers. A world without homeless men smearing your windshield with grimy rags at stoplights. A world without the constant wail of sirens. A world without neighbors who eye you with resentment. A world without D.

Willow tries to calm herself by focusing on more pleasant memories. Closing her eyes, she attempts to recreate the pleasant reverie of those long drives home from the lake when D was little. Joel is silent, eyes focused on the road ahead, as classical music plays on the car radio. D is asleep in the back seat, worn out after a day of running in the sand, skipping stones, and ignoring the stares from the pods of Chicago Russians on their beach towels. Or, she remembers with a smile, as D and I liked to call them, "those tattooed Stay Puft Marshmallow men."

She can't do it. Her mind keeps dragging her back to that awful day. D freaked at being removed from the corner room, but Joel convinced Willow they had to be firm. They needed to present a united front if they were going to put an end to D's "acting out." Willow managed to harden herself to her daughter's desperate pleas for a second chance, but she cringed when she heard those words coming out of her mouth.

"It's for your own good, sweetie. Someday you'll understand. You just have to trust us."

D became physically ill and locked herself in the bathroom. Joel took the door off the hinges when they heard her vomiting into the sink. Willow asked her husband to leave them alone, and he, with that damn shit-eating grin of his, asked if he should take the door with him? She found herself gripping one of the metal hinge pins he'd set on the counter and fighting the overwhelming urge to hit him with it. He must have read her mind because he disappeared without saying another word.

D knocked her hand away when she tried to wipe her chin. She was glad Joel wasn't there to see it. The two of them stood there in silence, D gripping the sink with both hands and staring bleakly into the mirror, Willow struggling to think of something to say that wasn't hopelessly anodyne. What she desperately wanted to do was to reach out and hold her daughter, to rock her in her arms like when she was a little girl, to let her know everything was going to be okay. But she was afraid. Afraid of being rejected. Afraid of...she didn't really quite know what.

Willow scolded herself, *Dammit! She's my child!*, and wrapped her arms around her daughter. There was no give. No sense of release. D's entire body was stiff and unyielding. Willow had never fully appreciated her daughter's size. There was a physicality about her that was intimidating. Scary even. Her own daughter. But she held on. She told herself she would never let go. Then, D threw up on her.

D waited until they were asleep and moved her things back into the corner room. She secured the door with the padlock from her school locker and refused to give them the combination. Even worse was the hand-lettered sign taped to the door: "No White People Allowed."

Willow kills the phone light when she senses movement in the hallway. She holds her breath as the sharp crack of splintering floorboards announces the beast's return. The T-Rex leans against the door, and the wood groans under the immense weight pressing against it. The creature is sniffing, snuffling, exploring, like a dog on the trail of a few crumbs. The demon could easily break through, but its efforts are tentative, almost delicate. Leathery scales scrape the wood like sandpaper. Jagged claws graze the surface in wide circles. The movement is delicate, almost tender—searching. Searching for what?

Then, the creature grows still. Willow listens as its breath pelts the door like the air brakes on a tractor trailer. Her mind is reeling. *Why doesn't it just plow through this pitifully thin barrier between us? Is the beast really here to hurt me? Maybe it's here to help? Maybe it's going to help me find D? Maybe D isn't really dead! Maybe this is all a bad dream.*

Maybe none of this is real. Maybe it's all in my mind. The intelligent thing to do, the logical thing to do, to prove it's not real, that it's all in my head, would be to open the goddamn door and see what's on the other side.

But the thought of doing such a thing is terrifying. She remembers those teeth. That gaping excavator bucket of a mouth. Those watchful eyes. No, the one thing she does know is that she has to stay where she is. *Someone will come for me. Someone has to come!*

The T-Rex on the other side of the door ROARS. Like a lion. Like a lion! Before pivoting and moving off with a thudding stride, clawed feet punching through the wood floorboards like jackhammers. She can hear it careening through the house, smacking into walls and pushing aside furniture as it goes. She wants to run away, but she's completely immobilized by fear. She knows it's going to come back. Or maybe something even worse. She's never getting out of here. She slides to the floor and crams herself into the space between the toilet and the wall.

⸻

Roy reaches the landing to find that the upstairs hall-way has been reduced to a narrow path through towering piles of hoarder treasures that must have taken decades to accumulate. The pulpy walls of mashed together bric-à-brac resemble a tunnel drilled through the center of a landfill. The compressed sedimentary layers are constructed from bulging shopping bags, cardboard boxes, clothing, suitcases, cast-off furniture, plastic storage tubs, and broken appliances.

Roy stops for a moment to prepare for what he knows lies ahead. "I got this," he says aloud, and strides forward into the gap. The greasy carpet beneath his feet has a sponge-like texture. Tendrils of soggy plaster hang from the ceiling like moss. The smell — a combination of piss, stale cigarette smoke, dead rodents, and fermenting roach spray — is overwhelming.

He slows to examine some of the objects embedded in this improbable urban dump. Bricked into the festering hoarder walls are lamps, clothing, quilts, cradles, work boots, books, bibles, magazines, newspapers, winter hats, church lady hats, fedoras, musical instruments, photo albums, frying pans, casserole dishes, and ordinary trash. It is the detritus of countless thousands of lives. The lives of people long gone and forgotten. And the mass of discarded material seems to be expanding even as he examines it.

At first, Roy moves easily through the dank canyon, with clearance off either shoulder. But, in a matter of steps, he is forced to turn sideways to get through the narrowing channel. The first four doorways he encounters are blocked solid with fossilized debris and clearly haven't been entered in years. Reaching the far end of the corridor, he finds that the doorway to the rear corner bedroom is clear. It's also padlocked.

A handmade sign hangs on the door stuck on a nail. Roy has a sharp intake of breath when he realizes what it is. *It's that same damn piece of paper from before!* He has to remind himself to breathe as he examines it with the flashlight. The sign is written in a shaky hand with a ballpoint pen that has ripped through the paper in places: "Keep Out! No drugs here! No money!"

Roy fingers the lock. He remembers what they found behind this door. She was still, somehow, making him coffee and grits every morning on an old hotplate. Squatters were cashing their SSI checks. White squatters. In what was then an all-Black neighborhood. When they found them—what was left of them—it was hard to even tell how many there had been.

He turns his attention back to the old lady behind the door. God knows how long she'd been living with her husband's body. If one of the neighbors hadn't called about that mess downstairs...

There's a window at the end of the corridor overlooking the street, and he can see the flashing blue lights from his cruiser reflecting off the tree canopy. He peers down at the patrol car, but there's no sign of the homeowner. "Damn! Slippery son of a bitch..."

The fierce glow from the conflagration on the west side means there's no help coming, so he turns his attention back to the door. The light leaking from underneath has the diffuse, stuttering quality of an open flame. He taps on the door. "Mrs. Ward? Are you in there?" He listens for a moment, but there is no response. He tries again, fingering the padlock.

"Did your husband do this, Mrs. Ward?" Leaning in closer, he detects the nauseating, sickly sweet odor of rotting meat left too long in a broken fridge. *Damn! That can only mean one thing: a dead body.*

Roy takes a step back. He tries to block out the grisly images they encountered on the other side of this door all those years before. The smell—from the dead, from the unwashed, from the plastic white bucket used for a toilet—hit you like a slap in the face as soon as you entered. The corpse was lying on the bed, shrunken and shrouded like a mummy beneath a festering quilt. Surrounding the corpse there was a circle of flickering candles, like the ones found at sidewalk shrines. A thin layer of powdered grit coated everything, giving the various objects in the room the appearance of grave offerings in a long-forgotten tomb chamber.

The room itself had been set up like a studio apartment with every square inch accounted for. There was a bookcase that served as a pantry with a hotplate on top. Two chairs crowded an old TV with rabbit ears, and a spindly legged card table was set with two bowls filled with what might have once been grits. Those grits, and a carefully folded yellowed newspaper, were still awaiting the deceased's attention in the next life. And then, huddled on the floor of the closet, there was a woman...

Before Roy can determine his next move, he is startled by the sound of something moving through the attic directly over his head. Cracks form in the plaster ceiling as what sounds like a damn water buffalo trundles across the attic floor overhead and crashes through a closed door or a wall and into the space above the corner bedroom. There is a brief flurry of frantic clawing as it attacks the attic floor. Then, it plunges through the ceiling on the other side of the door and hits the floor of the corner bedroom with the force of a steer falling off the back of a truck.

Roy unholsters the 9mm. He can hear the sounds of an animal snarling. *Now what?* He continues listening and realizes it must be a carnivore on the other side of the door, grunting as it feeds. What he's hearing is the grisly furor of a wild creature violently tearing through the flesh and bone of a carcass. *Much too big to be a dog,* he thinks. *A bear maybe?* Whatever it is, it's devouring whatever, whoever, lies dead inside that room.

Roy grips the gun in one hand and the flashlight in the other. He rocks back on his heels and prepares to put his shoulder to the door. Taking a deep breath, he visualizes himself as an invincible, armored knight in his Kevlar, webbing, belts, radio, Taser, holster, and service automatic. "Jesus, I believe in you. Jesus, I believe in everlasting life..."

His radio suddenly sparks to life. "Thank you, Jesus!" He sets the flashlight down on a stack of lumpen cardboard boxes and hits the mic switch. "Officer needs assistance. This is—" He barely gets the words out before an electronic shriek nearly shatters his eardrums. Startled, he kills the radio, his elbow toppling the flashlight from its precarious perch.

The flashlight hits the grungy carpet with a dull thud and proceeds to roll all the way down the hallway, projecting a whirling, kaleidoscopic halo of light across the hoarder wall as it goes. Then, he listens helplessly as it thumps, impossibly, one step at a time, all the way down the stairs.

There's no time to worry about the flashlight. The racket from the radio has aggravated whatever the hell is inside the room. The floor shakes beneath the footfalls of something enormous as it approaches the door. *It's not a bear,* Roy realizes; *it's a goddamn rhino!* He grips the 9mm with both hands and starts to back down the hallway. The entire house seems to be collapsing in on itself, and he has to force his way through the walls of debris that are pressing in on him as he goes.

Something slams into the bedroom door from the inside, and the padlock assembly is ripped away from the frame like a paper clip. The second blow shatters the door, causing the surrounding walls of fused-together hoarder dross to collapse in and bury the doorway.

Roy continues retreating down the corridor as something attempts to bull its way through the cascading mounds of wreckage. Then, a terrifying beast with glowing red eyes—all tooth and claw and gristle—emerges from the rubble. Roy can't believe what he's seeing. It's a big, fucking black dragon! Walking on two legs like a goddamned T-Rex or something!

The mass of debris continues to solidify behind Roy until he can't back up any further. He attempts to keep the gun pointed at the approaching apparition as the hoarder walls implode and he is pelted with a jagged meteor shower of bric-à-brac and trash.

Meanwhile, the beast, the entity, the whatever-the-goddamn-the-hell-it-is thing, is powering through the collapsing tunnel, bulldozing a compacted tidal wave of flotsam before it. Roy screams as the surging mass of debris slams into him like an avalanche. The last thing he remembers is losing his goddamn gun.

———

Willow awakens in the dark. Something woke her. Something shrill. A car alarm? Or was it someone screaming? Frantic at the possibility, she grabs the toilet tank with one hand, presses the other flat against the wall, and shimmies to her feet. *D? Is it D?*

No. Her body collapses like a punctured balloon, and she slides back down to the floor in defeat. *Of course it's not D. D's never coming back.*

The morning after D padlocked her bedroom door, Joel threatened to force it open with a crowbar. It wasn't easy, but Willow managed to calm him down and allow her to handle the escalating crisis with their daughter. She spoke to D through the locked door and got her to agree to family counseling. Well, let's just say she decided to interpret her daughter's stony silence as her assent to family counseling.

Once Joel left for work—without D—Willow relented and let her daughter move her things back into the corner room. She even allowed D to keep the lock in place so she could have her privacy. But the sign had to come down. That was non-negotiable. Willow had found the Black Princess placard online and hung it on the door in its place. D left it up, so she considered that another positive sign.

Joel wasn't happy when he learned of his wife's "unilateral surrender," but he didn't have much choice. For her part, Willow couldn't help but feel a little bit smug: she'd fixed things. It might be an ugly fix; it might be a peace treaty that left everyone bruised and unhappy, but it was a start. Hopefully, the worst was over. Hopefully, things were going to get better over time. If only she'd known how little time they had.

D didn't come down to dinner that night. Willow wanted to go up and get her, but Joel insisted she'd come down when she was good and hungry. She got up to go anyway, and he grabbed her arm so hard she had a bruise the next day. In the meantime—while her parents ate their dinner in stony silence—D packed a suitcase and slipped out of the house. She took Willow's car and didn't return. Not that night, or the next, or the next. They were going out of their minds with worry when she finally texted to say she was staying with friends and that she would be back in touch, "When you're ready to see me."

Their daughter didn't show up at school, and they couldn't figure out who the "friends" were that she was staying with. But they didn't report her as a runaway. They were afraid she'd be taken away. They were afraid of creating a permanent rupture with their daughter. They were afraid of how it would reflect on them.

Willow convinced herself that their daughter would come home once she sorted things out. But Joel—after seething for days—finally lost patience and called the police to report the unauthorized use of the car. Willow was horrified when she found out and demanded that he call the police immediately and tell them it was all a mistake. Joel refused. "It will teach her a lesson," he insisted. "Actions have consequences."

Willow was momentarily cowed by her husband's anger and waited for him to go upstairs to bed before calling to cancel the report. She told the police it was her car, and her daughter had her permission to use it. It was too late. D had already been pulled over. D was dead.

She closes her eyes again. She can stay here in the dark, wrapped in this gentle gauze of forgetfulness. *I can disappear. It'll be as if I no longer exist. No longer hurt. No longer miss D. No longer miss Joel. Do I miss Joel? The old Joel, maybe. When his moody silences gave him an air of mystery. When all the vagueness about his past was still somehow romantic. Like those veterans in the documentaries who you know really went through some heavy shit simply because they so gallantly refuse to talk about it. No. No more memories. She can forget her grief, her anger. She can even forget D, her love for her. Her fears for her. Her fear of her. No more memories.*

Then, she remembers. She straightens up so fast her head smacks the plaster wall behind her: *That thing! That monstrosity! It's coming back! That black T-Rex!* She fumbles around in the dark until she finds the phone. *I need to keep going,* she thinks. *I need to stay alive. I have to do it for D. I can still make sure D's life meant something. That she's remembered. I'll be more of an ally than I've ever been. A super ally.*

She tries to get her bearings in the dark. *Where am I? Where's the door?* She hits the flashlight app and shines the light around the room. She illuminates a section of the floor and runs her fingers over the vintage, black and white checkerboard tile with pride. *Pretty good job for a couple of rookies, huh? She and D ripped out the old, gross, multiple layers of linoleum. Hauled it to the dumpster in the alley and leveled the floor.*

When D went back to school, she carried on by herself. Picked out, cemented, and grouted the new tile. She's actually pretty good at tile grouting. A few YouTube videos. A little HGTV inspiration. Well, alright, a lot of YouTube videos. She tried hard to not let Joel see how much she was enjoying it. That he was right about...

Then she notices something else and leans down for a closer look. The tile grout she is so proud of is cracking. Not just the grout, hairline cracks have begun to etch the surface of the tiles themselves.

She cries out in terror as the house suddenly shifts on its foundation. The bathroom vanity begins to warp as the wall behind it ripples and swells. One of the lower cabinet doors bursts free from its hinges to reveal that the water supply pipe beneath the sink is pulling away from the wall. She watches as the pipe dances and writhes, contorting like a snake, until it separates completely from the wall. She cringes, expecting to get doused, but no water comes out.

There is more movement in the dark recess beneath the sink, and Willow shines the light into the narrow cavity. The ragged hole in the wall is a foot in diameter now and growing. A bulbous mass of tendrils is emerging from the punctured wallboard and wood lathe, like the fibrous tangle of guts and intestines spilling out from the insides of a butchered deer.

The fleshy beanstalk coils quickly expand to fill the space, and the thin cabinet walls begin to crack under the strain. The rising mass of sinew and meat tears the quartz countertop from its brackets, and Willow watches in horror as the lumpen mess begins to emerge from the ruined vanity like some monstrous hatchling.

She scrambles on her hands and knees to the door just as the sink and quartz countertop crash to the floor behind her. She reaches up to grab the doorknob, but it's jammed shut, and she realizes that the entire weight of the house is pressing down on the doorframe with crushing force. Before she can react, the hinges give way, and the door falls on top of her. A maelstrom of rubble cascades down on top of the door and pins her to the floor.

J oel is at the side door. *It's locked! And why wouldn't it be?* It was locked the last time he circled the house. Just like the front door. And the back door. *Where the hell is that cop? Where is Willow?*

He steps back for a better look at the house. His home, his former home perhaps, is a steep-sided urban butte with a brick facade and the shapes of windows chiseled into the cliff face. He pushes through the side gate and into the yard. He immediately stumbles over something rigid protruding from the ground, but a soggy pile of trash bags breaks his fall. He looks around the rubble-filled yard in consternation. *What the hell happened back here? Who dumped all this shit? And what the hell happened to our garden?*

At first, he thinks he's tripped over one of their landscape border stones, but they seem to have disappeared completely from the yard. The object he tripped over appears to be the top end of a large stone marker or gravestone that has risen out of the soil. He wipes away the dirt, but the inscription has either been worn away or is on the part of the marker still in the ground. Joel climbs to his feet and brushes himself off. I haven't got time for this shit.

Joel goes out the back gate and through the alley. He stands on the sidewalk, momentarily transfixed by the light bar atop the police cruiser with its strobing blue beacons. Then, hearing the rumble of an engine somewhere off in the distance, he peers through the tunnel beneath the rail embankment and sees the taillights of a garbage truck about a block further down the street. The squat vehicle is hunkered down like some armored, dystopian beast as its mechanical appendage reaches out to grab a trash bin from the street. There is a brief clatter of cascading rubbish and breaking glass as the skeletal arm shakes the contents into the truck's hopper bed before slamming the bin back onto the pavement.

Joel hurries through the underpass in the direction of the garbage truck. Maybe this guy will know what's going on... Emerging on the other side, his hands and face tingle briefly as he passes through a breezy flutter of energy as diffuse as a gauzy spider web. He jogs after the truck as it moves on to the next bin. Then he stops and watches in horror as the truck transforms into a giant lizard...No, not a lizard, an insect, a gargantuan, beetle-like creature with twin pincers that lash out to skewer its helpless prey and cram it into the gaping maw at its back.

Joel turns and runs. The houses all around him began to bloat, snuffing out the lights in their windows as they swell, until they are a pitch-dark, quivering reef of lumpen tumors pressing in on him from both sides. By the time he reaches the other side of the railway berm, the truck has disappeared into the gloom. The street is silent again. The houses on either side of the street are once again composed of brick, cement, and asphalt roofing tiles.

His own house is shrouded in darkness. Then, Joel spots the dim glow behind the quartz-like surface of the window in D's room. *Dammit! I told her: no open flames in the house.* Then he remembers: D is dead.

Joel beats on the front door of the house with the crowbar until he's completely winded. The door, like the rest of the house, has fossilized into a substance the density of cast iron, and his hands are beginning to ache from hammering at the unyielding surface. He stumbles as he retreats down the porch steps and topples backward on his ass into the tall grass. Then, stunned by what he's seeing, he uses the crowbar like a cane to lever himself to his feet.

The house has begun to wobble as the ground beneath it liquefies. The drainpipes and gutters have morphed into fleshy capillaries, throbbing with some primal current as they wrap the house in a grim stranglehold. They seem to be the only thing holding the structure together as the exterior walls undulate and swell while a geyser of molten, lava-like muck emerges from somewhere deep inside the earth and rises steadily through the interior. The fiery miasma ignites the window shades and curtains on contact, then quickly snuffs out those same flames as it completely fills the house.

The glistening sludge, now packing every square inch of the structure, churns and boils, as if undergoing some sort of chemical reaction. Joel, half expecting it to blow through the roof like an erupting volcano, backs even further away from the house. The stout walls manage to contain the explosive agitation, but the exterior bricks glow with the bristling heat of a kiln.

Then, the entire structure begins to convulse. The windows shatter, venting rifled beams of light and heat into the night. Walls tumble. The roof caves in. The cadaverous framework of timbers, lathe, brick, steel, and plaster writhes, bends, twists, and deforms, until the whole mess collapses in on itself.

***

Willow is wedged in tight. Her right shoulder is jammed hard against the tile floor while her other shoulder bears the weight of the collapsed rubble covering the door. *Lucky,* she thinks, *I didn't have time to react and try to catch myself. Probably would have broken my wrist.*

She wants to turn over, to take the agonizing pressure off her shoulders, but she knows that the weight pushing down on the door will pin her face-down against the floor if she tries to shift her position. She looks around for something to prop up the door, so the weight is no longer directly on her. She can feel the hard, polished edge of the sink pressing against her back, but there's no way she can twist around to face it, much less maneuver it into position to prop up the door.

The entire house shudders again, and Willow panics as the weight of the door presses down sharply on her. Then, suddenly, the house shifts again, almost like the intake of a breath, and the door rises just enough to free her shoulder. Willow curls up in a fetal position and waits to see what happens next. There is a strange thrum in the air, and the unseen mass of rubble surrounding her is throbbing and pulsating like a living organism. The door, inches above her head now, is vibrating. She reaches out to touch it but quickly draws back when she finds the wood to be warm and palpitating, like something alive.

The door bears down on her again, but now it has taken on the consistency of raw meat and begins to wrap itself around her like a giant, greasy tongue. She can feel the entire weight of the house, soft and deadly, pressing down on her. She wonders if it would be best to just surrender, to let the house take her, to finally be at peace.

Then, she hears it. The beast is somewhere close. Its deep-throated growl is the rumble of a diesel excavator, alternately revving and stalling as it burrows through the compacted rubble. Willow rolls onto her stomach, and the door moves with her, pressing down on her back with the weight of a child's wading pool filled with water. She looks for a way out, but the mounds of refuse surrounding her have congealed into one solid surface.

Rotating in place, with her cheek polishing the tile floor as she goes, she finds a small opening where the door used to be. The crushing weight on her body is making it hard to breathe as she claws at the loose rubble blocking her way. Pushing aside an old toaster and a bent ironing board, she wiggles through a gap in the throbbing wall of her prison and emerges on the other side like a cork from a bottle.

Willow finds herself in the hallway and lies there for a moment, reveling in the ability to breathe again. She tries to stand, but the corridor has shrunk as new growth continues to emerge on all sides. The walls of the narrow passage consist of hoarder debris that has fused together into coarse layers with the texture of quilted concrete. Every surface is continuously undulating, throbbing, and swelling as the house continues its mysterious evolution. Somewhere in the distance she can hear the muffled exertions of the beast as it bullies its way through an adjoining shaft.

Willow moves forward at a crouch, wading through the bog of soggy books, twisted strollers and cardboard boxes of clothing turning to mush, partially blocking the passage. Somewhere behind her, she hears a triumphant roar as the beast bursts through the wall of an adjoining passage and into hers.

The sounds of the beast grow closer as it struggles to force its savage bulk through the chaotic passage. Willow plows ahead with frantic energy, fighting her way through the wreckage of small appliances and plastic trash bags. Then, she trips and falls flat on her face. Clawing through the fibrous muck as she struggles to her hands and knees, Willow's hand closes around a hard, metal object. She pulls it close for a better look and realizes it's a gun.

Did Joel have a gun in the house? The possibility makes her angry. *How dare he!* She starts to push the weapon to the side in disgust. But then, with the beast's roar echoing out from the passage behind her, she changes her mind. No, *this is a sign,* she thinks. *This is providence!*

She wraps both hands around the grip and raises the weapon. Holding this lethal tool makes her feel something she has not experienced in a very long time. She feels powerful. *This can be about me,* she thinks. *I can be the hero. I'll no longer be running scared in my own house. To hell with Joel. To hell with Jacob. I'm going to take my house back! I'm going to take my life back!*

Pointing the weapon at an unseen target, she shouts into the darkness. "I am goddamn Ripley! This is my house! My goddamn house! I'm not leaving! I'm never leaving!"

She hears the beast approaching, smashing everything in its path as it forces its way through the narrow tunnel. Clasping the gun in both hands, Willow swivels on her haunches to face the creature.

The T-Rex has been forced to move through the tight space with its head lowered nearly to the ground. The prehistoric jaws open wide as it approaches. The gaping mouth fills the tunnel, with densely stacked columns of chisel-like teeth crowding the cavernous gullet. Willow points the gun but can't bring herself to pull the trigger. Then, she is struck with a blast of fetid air as the massive jaws snap shut directly in front of her with the finality of a casket.

The beast moves forward until the hatchback of a snout is pressing right up against the barrel of the gun. Trembling, she raises the gun until it is pointing directly into one of the dinner-plate-sized eyes. "I'll shoot. I will. This is my house! You need to get the hell out of my house!"

Up close, she can see that the T-Rex's skin has the rugged texture of a petrified tree trunk. The flesh around the eyes is cratered and pockmarked, and the look in those eyes is one of deep sadness. Something about that gaze, ancient and wise, has her flashing on a story she saw on Facebook. About a diver, pummeled by the massive snout of a blue whale and fearing for her life, until she realized the behemoth was trying to save her from an approaching shark.

As Willow's eyes meet the creature's searching gaze, she realizes she is, somehow, being asked to lower the gun. Despite her anger, she wants to lower the gun. But she is paralyzed with fear by the mere proximity to this massive, black entity. Then, the creature's giant muzzle, with all the soft, persuasive power of an aggressive parade float, pushes Willow to the side. She huddles in a cavity in the wall as the beast surges past her, the powerful hind legs propelling it through the passage like a grizzled tunnel boring machine.

Willow can only watch as it glides by, marveling at the tangle of scars, grooves, and gouges crisscrossing the pebbled hide and chronicling a violent history measured in eons. When the beast is gone, Willow lowers the gun. Then inexplicably, for no reason she can fathom, she begins to sob.

Joel stands on the front lawn staring at the place where his house used to stand. The wreckage of the roof is the flayed hide of a grotesque beast covering the pulsating husk that is all that remains of the structure. Then, as Joel watches in astonishment, the sinewy shroud of shingles and tarpaper begins to rise as the mound of rubble beneath begins to reconstitute itself. Joel backs up all the way into the street as a 3,000 - square-foot larva emerges from the brick and offal cocoon and slowly transforms itself into a house again.

Joel realizes he's hearing sirens. A lot of sirens. *Thank God*, he thinks. *The cavalry is here.*

Roy is tumbling, spinning, helpless, ass over elbows, in the middle of a deluge. Or a tidal wave, maybe. Or maybe he's goddamn Dorothy inside the tornado. But this sure as hell ain't Kansas. Then, he's hit with another wave of...something. Something that has him whipping and whirling like a wet noodle in a storm drain. No, *it's a damn flood*, he tells himself. *Biblical even. And me without a damn ark!*

Then he realizes, for some inexplicable reason, he's not afraid. Not even a little bit. It's all somehow invigorating. Cleansing even. Like a baptism. *Yeah, like one of those full immersion baptisms my in-laws—*

It all ends in one hell of a hard-ass landing. *Story of my damn life*, Roy thinks, doing his best to execute a tuck and roll as he skids across a hard floor and slams into a concrete wall. Roy slowly uncoils himself from the fetal position he's assumed and determines he's unhurt. It takes a few more seconds for his eyes to get accustomed to the dark. Meanwhile, he feels around on the floor for his gun. Nothing.

Once his eyes adjust, he discovers he's back in the basement. The pulsating mounds of rubble and trash have welded themselves into a dense thicket of stout tendrils, rooting the house above his head to the earth beneath his feet. They are expanding at a rapid pace, and it's clear they will soon completely fill the space. The concrete floor has turned to something with the consistency of soggy oatmeal in places, and he realizes he has to hurry before it all liquefies.

Roy presses his back up against the wall and struggles to his feet. He spots the basement stairs through the tangle of roots and sets off in that direction. As he squeezes his body through the narrowing gaps, Roy realizes that these strange forms are vibrating, humming with life, alive. If he stops moving, if he remains still, he can hear the muffled, whispered voices of tens of thousands of forgotten souls. But he has to keep moving.

The walls of the house have formed themselves into the hard outer shell of a monstrous cocoon. And a new entity is incubating inside that cocoon, rooted deep into the earth, feeding on and drawing energy from the bone and the ash, the grief and the pain, the joys and the hopes of countless lost generations.

Roy presses his hands against his ears in a fruitless attempt to shut it all out as he tries to bull his way through the morass. He stops short when he realizes the floor between him and the stairs has become a bubbling, churning quagmire. He's trapped—there's no way forward, and the burgeoning forest of tendrils is pressing in on him from all sides, squeezing him in a vise-like grip.

Then, he sees a flat stone oozing up through the muck. Others follow, emerging from the sludge to form a rough series of stepping stones between him and the stairs. He moves forward, stepping gingerly from stone to stone. Some are stable, allowing him to find his balance and brace for the next step. Others sink as soon as his toe presses down on them, forcing him to leap perilously onto the next.

Roy reaches the staircase and sprawls across the stairs, pressing his face gratefully against the rough wood riser. He hears a sucking sound behind him and turns to see the pathway of stones sink back beneath the mire. *Funny*, he thinks to himself as he rises and heads up the stairs. *Kinda looked like tombstones.*

The house is tilting and rolling like a ship at sea as Willow careens from window to window—living room, dining room, kitchen, front hallway. She holds the gun pressed against her hip as she peers through each window in turn, trying to make sense of what she sees. The house is surrounded by a necklace of flashing red and blue light bars. There are police cars lined up on the side street, on the street in front of the house, in the alley. There's a patrol car sitting on the front lawn of the house next door. There are even police cars on the rail embankment.

She moves away from the windows, retreating to the archway between the living and dining rooms. From where she's standing, she can see the strobing mosaic of red and blue lights through the windows on three sides. One thing for sure, she thinks: That T-Rex is going exactly nowhere with all those cops out there.

Things are beginning to calm down. The occasional stuttering tremor, like the aftershocks of an earthquake, continues to rattle her nerves, but the house is once again on solid ground. The lights don't work, but the strobing emergency flashers outside provide enough illumination for her to see that the rooms have returned to their original dimensions. The debris she was forced to wade through is gone, and there are no longer any tunnels bored through masses of hoarder trash.

But the details are wrong. It's hard to tell in the dim light, but the art on the walls, the carpet, the fixtures, and the furniture placement are all different. It's as if someone came into the house and did a complete makeover while she was asleep.

The necklace of police cars begins to move, slowly circling the house. As she watches, the orbiting vehicular satellites pick up the pace, spinning faster and faster, until the ring of red and blue lights atop the police cars merge into a blurred magenta streak. Willow squeezes her eyes shut. She needs to hold it together. She has to find the beast.

I need to get my damn house back. She repeats it to herself like a mantra. *My house! My house! My house! Then she hears it.* There's someone in the back hallway. By the side door. Right by the entrance leading to the basement stairs.

Willow remembers the gun in her hand. She needs to get her house back. To do that, she needs to find the beast. *I won't hesitate this time. And if I kill it,* she assures herself, *everything will return to the way it was before. Well, almost; without D, of course.*

Joel is standing on the neatly trimmed front lawn that could double as a putting green. He winces when he reaches up to hold his broken glasses in place and his hand tags his wounded ear. He's staring at what was his house, which has transformed itself in front of his eyes. The roof looks fairly new. The brickwork, the gutters, the wood trim, are all original and well maintained. The front door is beautiful, and the missing leaded-glass window Willow was never able to source is intact.

In fact, the house appears to have been completely renovated. More accurately, it looks as if the house never needed to be renovated. It was never subjected to decades of abuse, never carved into multiple units. Never abandoned and stripped by scavengers. Instead, the house, solid and well cared for, has sheltered generations of families. Through good times and bad. Mostly good, it appears.

There is a train rumbling by on the berm behind the house, mostly tank cars. The passing train is creating very little vibration, so Joel assumes the tank cars must be empty. Behind the moving train, to the west, there are stars in the nighttime sky. And there is no fire.

Joel turns his attention to the semi-circle of cops facing him. *What do you call a group of cops?* he wonders? *A pack? A pride? A herd? A scrum?* Their stern faces are Black, white, brown, and Asian. There are men, women, and someone, as far as he can tell, of indeterminate gender. Joel never realized the police department had such diversity.

The porch light reveals the residents of the house gathered on the porch to watch the little drama playing out on their front lawn. It's a Black family. There's mom, dad, teenage son, pre-teen daughter, and another daughter who looks to be about five. They could be one of those picture-perfect families from the TV commercials, he thinks. Except, those families are always mixed race these days.

A cop—looks like the boss cop, a sergeant or something—is asking if they can go inside and talk. Dad's not listening. Instead, he's angrily jabbing a finger at Joel. "He's been running around all night, beating on our windows. We don't know him. Never saw that man before in my life. He's damn lucky I don't own a gun."

Mom, aggrieved, chimes in. "Says the house belongs to him. I grew up in this house. That man needs help."

The officer gestures, and they start to go inside the house. "That's alright. We'll sort it out."

The teenage boy holding the door for the others looks to the cops now closing in on Joel. "Y'all be careful. These old white guys, they got all kinds 'a guns and stuff."

All Joel can think of in his frazzled state of mind as he's handcuffed is: *Old?* Then, he notices that the youngest daughter, the last one through the door, has a toy dinosaur figure dangling from her hand. A black toy dinosaur. A

T-Rex. That brings back a memory for Joel. *Wait. Didn't D...?*

"Hey!" He's suddenly on the ground, with the wind knocked out of him, his eyeglasses splintering beneath the boot of a nearby cop.

———

Roy grips the knob on the side door but hesitates. He can't leave without his service weapon. *I need to find my damn gun.* He can hear the hub-hub of voices coming from the front of the house. *Now what?* He wonders. At the same instant, he senses something behind him and turns to see a white woman pointing his own gun at him. He holds both hands in front of him, palms up, in a calming gesture.

"Mrs. Ward?"

She doesn't respond.

"Ma'am?"

She just stands there, pointing the gun at his head. One side of her face is scraped raw. Her long ivory hair is clumped into one big, knotted snarl, giving her an air of loopy derangement. She's trembling, staring at him through her grimy eyeglasses like he's some creature from another planet. She could be in shock. Whatever it is, she's clearly not all there.

Roy speaks with the practiced calm of a man who's seen more than his share of tense situations. "It's okay. It's over. Whatever the hell that was, it's done."

He holds his hand out for the weapon. Her finger is resting on the Glock's trigger release. "Please be careful. Take your finger off the trigger. Nice and easy now."

Her finger remains poised over the trigger, but she lowers the gun slightly. "I miss D."

He doesn't know what the hell she's talking about, but that doesn't matter right now. "I know. I'm sorry." He takes a careful step forward and extends his hand for the gun.

She's staring at the gun like it's some immense insect latched onto the end of her arm. "I've never even held a gun before."

"I know. It's okay," he reassures her. He moves a step closer. His fingers are almost touching the weapon.

Roy freezes as the probing beams of several flashlights pierce the kitchen window to his right. He looks over to see the face of a uniformed cop peering through the glass. A white cop. He's immediately joined by a young Black cop, and Roy has an instant flash of recognition. *It's that kid. The one with the dumbass baseball cap. All grown up. What the…?*

Behind Roy, another cop is trying the door, but it's locked. Roy calls over his shoulder. "It's okay. I'm a cop. I got this. Stand the fuck down!"

Then, from the direction of the kitchen window, he hears someone shout, "Gun!"

Roy hears the door being kicked in behind him. He doesn't need to think very hard to work this one out. *Cops coming through the door hot. Crazy white lady pointing a gun.* He hits the ground hard, grateful for the rough cushioning of the body armor. Cradling his head in his arms, he shouts, "Noooooo!"

He already knows it's too late.

Officer Roy Sermon suddenly feels very, very old.

Joel is flat on his stomach, face down in the grass, hands cuffed behind his back. He can smell the nitrogen in the freshly applied fertilizer. He can hear even more sirens. He remembers those times as a small boy, lying awake in his bed at night and listening to the sound of distant sirens. Somehow, that piercing wail in the dead of night was comforting.

It meant that people, serious people, grown-up people, would be awake and taking care of business while he slept. It made him feel safe and secure in the darkness. It was a sign that all was right with the world.

Joel hears gunshots and realizes he needs to do something. He needs to make sure Willow is okay. Not now though. Someone's knee is pressing down on his neck.

The End

ABOUT PETER O'KEEFE

Peter O'Keefe is a writer and filmmaker, born and raised in Detroit, now living in Racine, Wisconsin. His first novel Counted With the Dead—a reimagining of Frankenstein set in late-90s Detroit—was released by Grendel Press in 2024. Peter has worked in episodic television and feature films and written TV movies for German networks.

His narrative short films have screened at a variety of film festivals and Peter's documentary about visual artists in the American Midwest, "Dreaming In Public, Making Art In the Real World" was awarded a Chicago Regional Emmy. His short stories have appeared in various literary and online journals and anthologies.

Dark Disturbances- 2024 Uncomfortably Dark Author Sampler Anthology.

Dark Asylum – 2025 Uncomfortably Dark Author Sampler Anthology.

<u>NOVELS & COLLECTIONS</u>
EPISODES OF VIOLENCE by David Bernstein
DREAMWHISPERS by M Ennenbach
CREMATED REMAINS by M Ennenbach
CUCKOO by M Ennenbach
OLD TOO SOON by Brian Bowyer
BLACKOUT: MICROPOETRY by Brian Bowyer
INNOCENCE ENDS by Nikolas P. Robinson
HAVE A BLAST by Nikolas P. Robinson
COME OUT & PLAY by Patrick Tumblety
ROADS TO RUIN by Brian Bowyer
SUBJECT A by M Ennenbach
OIOS LYKOS by M Ennenbach
STORYSLAVE by Brian Bowyer
VERUM MALUM by Michael R. Collins
PENNYROYAL TEA by Aaron Lebold
THE SHERIFF OF SALEM by Aaron Lebold
GENOCIDE by Aaron Lebold
QUARANTINE by Aaron Lebold
BLASPHEMY by Aaron Lebold
SLENDER BONES IN SACRED SOIL by Fredrick Niles
THIS IS HOW A VILLAIN IS MADE by Amanda Headlee
COFFEE SHOP by Aaron Lebold
ONE FRIGHT ONLY by Patrick Tumblety

Order signed copies and limited-edition hardcovers from the shop:
https://www.uncomfortablydark.com/shop

Join our Patreon for free books, merch, and more!
https://www.patreon.com/user/membership?u=1223133
0&view_as=patron

www.ingramcontent.com/pod-product-compliance
Lightning Source LLC
Chambersburg PA
CBHW030007010826

48973CB00009B/2701